I FOUND HIM DEAD

I Found Him Dead

BY GALE GALLAGHER

WILDSIDE PRESS

I Found Him Dead

Published by Wildside Press LLC
www.wildsidepress.com

I FOUND HIM DEAD

1.
SHE sat on a bench in the reception room, genuine honey blonde and beautiful. I guessed her age at thirty-five, but she was playing it younger. The round baby-neck blouse, the glowing, artless make-up, the natural-tint nails were all too carefully right. She wore a six-carat diamond but no wedding ring. She glanced up when I opened the door and her blue eyes met mine levelly for a moment. I knew that behind that carefully cool, appraising glance there was fear.

Without speaking, I went through to the inner office closing the door. Patsy Higgins, my secretary-assistant, was tucked between her typewriter and the monitor switchboard. She made frantic signals toward the waiting room. I got the general idea and nodded. Then Patsy closed the little information window between us and the reception room, so our visitor outside wouldn't hear.

I dropped my sassy new spring sailor hat with my purse on the file cabinet and glanced quickly over the mail. Patsy waited impatiently, finally thrust a new record card under my nose.

Dawn Ferris, it said. Actress. Home address: 502 East 88th Street, Manhattan. Business address: Radio City.

"That's her," Patsy babbled. Patsy's unprogressive

parents never heard of orthodontry, so her projecting front teeth resulted in a lisp when she spoke and an expression of childish surprise at all times. However, she is a good kid and, at that moment, radiated sheer ecstasy.

"I recognized her voice, Gale. Right away. The minute she came to the window and asked to see you."

"She's not our first customer," I said with deliberate, bubble-bursting flatness.

"But she's Dawn Ferris, the radio actress. I listened to her in the summertime when I was on vacation from school, and Mamma still hears her every day."

"The Katharine Cornell of the ether!"

"Gale!" Patsy was outraged. "In the first place, she's Ann Preston, Woman Physician. That's ten-thirty every morning. And she's Laura in *The Uphill Way*, at three in the afternoon, except week ends. Once you hear her . . ."

Bobby-sox stuff, I thought, listening to Patsy rave because a real live radio star had walked into the office. "Hold on to your emotions, Patsy," I said lightly. "Skip tracers can't afford them."

"But she . . . she's in trouble."

Patsy was appealing personally for a friend in distress. "It had better be good," I said. "Dragging me away from Maxine's before my nails were dry."

Patsy looked approvingly at my manicure with a lacquer optimistically called Rosy Future. My long oval nails were Patsy's special envy. She approved the color, assured me they were thoroughly dry, and reported on the morning's phone calls.

I was only half listening to her. It was my turn now

to think of the woman in the reception room. Patsy really had something. I rarely rated visits from prominent actresses. They didn't lose the kind of things that the Acme Investigating Bureau, G. K. Gallagher, principal, hunted down.

That look, with fear gnawing at the edges, was still there when I opened the door again. She was gazing straight ahead, as though her thoughts—and her terrors —fastened on some invisible point in the future. When I spoke her name, Dawn Ferris rose swiftly, recovered her poise practically in mid-air. Her professional smile blotted out the fear.

"I . . . must have been daydreaming." Her voice was deep, modulated, resonant. "I hope Miss Gallagher hasn't been detained. I'm due at the studio at two."

"I'm Gale Gallagher."

"Oh!"

I was used to the flash of surprise. People expect me to be fat and fifty, the police-matron type. Dawn Ferris murmured apologies for her mistake as I led her past Patsy into my private office.

We'd done a nice job partitioning our small office space. There was the plain, bird-cage size reception room, the utilitarian inner office, and then my office. I had spread myself on that. It was finished in three tones of brown, my favorite color, with highlights of yellow, and I think it's becoming to me.

Seated at my desk, the wide window overlooking Fifth Avenue behind me, I can face my clients and also see my pride and joy on the opposite wall—an original Thomas Benton landscape. The picture is a kind of quiet friend. In a crazy way, I like to think that it and

5

I together listen to the stories—the sordidness, the heartbreak, and all the trouble poured out in that room—and still keep our perspective. It made a fine backdrop as Dawn Ferris faced me across the desk, the light from the window full upon her. She smiled, an easy, tender, but somehow desperate smile.

She said, "I heard about you from Roy Selig, my agent. You handled some work for him."

"Oh, yes, I remember that case. The young actor who got discouraged and left town. Then Mr. Selig landed him a movie contract on an old screen test, and couldn't find him. It isn't often I get a chance to hunt people down to—give them good news."

"I suppose not. Roy said you were very resourceful and followed every angle."

"Nice of him to recommend me."

"But he didn't. He merely happened to mention you. I mean, he didn't send me here. Nobody knows I came. It mustn't become known. Only . . . I need . . ."

She hesitated as if she were not sure what she needed, like a patient who believes she has some dreadful disease but when face to face with the physician doubts the reality of her fears. For a moment she looked past me through the wide window to the towering buildings of Manhattan. "I want you to find a little girl." She spoke the words flatly, as if it were a first reading at rehearsal and she were trying them on for size.

"Miss Ferris," I said, "this sounds like a police case. We trace persons who run out on hotel bills, flighty wives who traipse off with the milkman, husbands who duck financial responsibility; but children—lost children . . ."

6

She leaned forward on the desk, her slim white hands clasped together tightly. "You don't understand. This girl is—my daughter."

"Your daughter—you lost her?"

"Miss Gallagher." She hesitated, looking straight at me. "I . . . I gave her away," she finished, so softly it was almost a whisper.

She was in trouble. No amount of make-up or acting ability could hide that. But a woman, I was thinking, doesn't give up her child, not if she can help it, not for any reason. I'm not a mother. My own mother died when I was born, so I never had that kind of love. I did have the wonderful sweeping love of my father, Patrolman James Patrick Gallagher, one of the finest men in the New York Police Department. It was he, I always say, who gave me my start in crime. But this mother love—I was still sure about it even if I didn't know it firsthand—was something one didn't part with easily.

Something of my emotions must have shown in my face because Dawn Ferris said, "I suppose you can't understand how a mother with half a heart could give away a child. But—it was a different world in 1933."

"Fourteen years," I said slowly. "And only now you've decided to look her up?"

"I haven't any right, even now, because that was part of the bargain. You see . . . I gave her for adoption."

That was different, but it still rasped in my mind even though I realized I had none of the details, none of the reasons. Probably it's my background. I grew up in a section of Manhattan that would now be called a low-income neighborhood. We had a little house, but all about us were old-law tenements, crowded and dirty. For most of our neighbors it was a struggle to pay the rent. Yet the women kept their kids. In and out of marriage, they kept them.

"If your child was placed for adoption, with your consent, through legal channels . . ." I was trying to be impartial, "you forfeited all right to her. Agencies will not reveal names of adopting parents. And after fourteen years . . ."

"I realize all that. I was resigned to it. It was my loss. I'm not proud of my personal history, Miss Gallagher."

I offered her a cigarette. She took it. I held the match for her, then lit my own.

"So many things have happened," she said. "A whole set of things, and all at once. For one, I—I'm to be married next month . . . to Geoffrey Wilton."

"Geoffrey Wilton." The name sounded a buzzer in my mind. "I seem to remember something recently—in *Time* magazine."

"He formed a new theatrical producing company. He's an engineer by profession, and made plane parts during the war." Shadows of anxiety clouded her eyes. "I haven't told him about my daughter. It wasn't only that I was ashamed, but it's been so long that I considered it a closed book. Sometimes I feel as if it all happened to someone else."

"So whatever your reasons for reopening this thing, you can't tell him about the girl now."

"How could I explain at this late date? I've known him two years. I . . . we . . . love each other."

"Does he know you were married? Or—were you?"

She nodded quickly, almost eagerly defensive. To the world Dawn Ferris was an adult woman, a successful

8

actress, but within herself a frightened child, the fear more fully revealed as she began talking rapidly.

"I married Eddie Wells in Topeka in 1931. I was twenty and doing a single in roadhouses. We teamed up, Eddie and Ethel Wells." She smiled, brightly reminiscent for the moment. "We made a fairly good double, and got some bookings on the five-a-day. But vaudeville was dying and things went very badly for us. Soon I realized it wasn't merely the times. It was also Eddie." She hesitated, then added softly, "He was emotionally unstable."

I would have bet she didn't know that phrase in 1931. "Unstable—in what way?"

She continued carefully, as though putting certain thoughts into words for the first time. "He wanted everything he saw, like a greedy child. Always chasing a rainbow—in the next town. He was completely dishonest. I don't mean that he was a thief—Eddie didn't have the courage to steal. He knew every angle to beat a board bill, promote a loan, or dodge a creditor. He was constantly in debt, constantly in trouble."

Eddie Wells sounded like the subject of most of my searches—the skip tracer's delight. I let Dawn continue, though the first quick brightness vanished. She went on with a visible effort, her mouth pinched at the corners, making little lines in her neck that showed her age.

"Then I was going to have a baby. I stayed in the act as long as possible. Eddie couldn't get bookings as a single on the road, but he thought things might be better in New York. We hitchhiked east." She looked at me with that quick level trick she had. "Do you remember the depression, Miss Gallagher?"

I shook my head. That was after Dad died. I was tucked in a convent school all through those years.

`"Then you don't know fear," Dawn Ferris said flatly. "Now, with money in the bank, I can't really believe that anyone in this city could starve, but we almost did." The truth of it was in her eyes. "We lived in a miserable furnished room and were always behind in the rent. It was years before I could hear footsteps on stairs without shivering. There was never enough to eat—frequently nothing at all. The baby was almost due and I'd had no medical care. Eddie disappeared and had been gone for two weeks. I wasn't sure he'd ever come back. . . ."

Watching her closely, I was trying to vision this sophisticated, perfectly groomed creature as the starving wife of a no-good chiseler. She realized the contrast, filled in the picture.

"I was very young and really inexperienced. I was hungry and desperately frightened when a girl in the house told me about Dr. Wurber."

Famous last words! How many Dr. Wurbers there had to be in the world!

"He had a private nursing home in the West Sixties. He placed babies with only wealthy or prominent families, especially those who wanted infants in a hurry without too much red tape. The baby had to be legitimate and healthy."

She shivered slightly, remembering. "Dr. Wurber was a horrible little man, but he said he would keep me at the hospital for that last month, feed me—which was so terribly important—deliver the baby, and give me two hundred dollars."

The old traffic in lives.

"What did I have to give her?" She went on. "Birth in a charity ward—and after that, what? We were broke, homeless. I had no people. This way she'd be taken care of. She'd have wealth, security; and a family to love her."

I tried to keep my emotions out of this. I was getting as bad as Patsy. "You had to have your husband's consent."

"I got that. Dr. Wurber found Eddie—strange how he could do it so quickly. He was a singing waiter in a beer garden out near Freeport. He went very sentimental when the doctor approached him. He actually cried, but he agreed to sign the papers—if I'd split the two hundred with him. I did."

The lines of her scarlet lips were tight. "Dr. Wurber said the baby was a girl, but I never saw her. He assured me it was easier that way. I never saw Eddie again, either."

I walked to the window, looked down at the taxis and busses crawling on the street below. You still haven't any answers, Gale, my girl, I told myself. She hasn't yet said what she came here to say. She's dodging, trying to get away—from something. I could hear it in this carefully edited version of her life, see it in the nervous motions of her hands as she took a handkerchief from the large purse on her lap.

"I never saw him again, but Eddie kept track of me. I don't know how; but then he was always amazingly efficient when he chose to be. At first I went into burlesque. It was the only job open." Her mouth curved, disdainful of her memories. "For one season I was billed as the gun moll of a notorious gangster. I changed my

11

name twice, but somehow Eddie always knew, and let me know it. He asked for money—small amounts, then."

"Did you send him any money?"

"No, never. I answered only one of his letters. That was in 1937, after I got my big break in radio. I was in Chicago when somebody discovered my speaking voice. I studied drama, landed my first good radio parts. As soon as I could afford it, I got a divorce on the grounds of desertion. It was his next letter that I answered. I told him I was free and asked him to leave me alone. I did get fewer letters, but the demands were bigger. In 1942 I came to New York under contract for the two big spots I have now. I didn't hear from Eddie again. I thought I was really free."

How many times have I heard that line! *I thought I was free. I thought I could put the past behind me.* Only you never can. You and the past are one.

"And now Eddie," I said, "has decided to return."

"I had a letter from him last Monday." She fumbled in the smoothly expensive purse, handed me a dog-eared envelope, with a Grand Central, New York, post-office cancelation. The envelope was addressed in an old-fashioned, flowery script, to Dawn Ferris, care of the broadcasting company.

"That his handwriting?" I asked.

She nodded. "Eddie has very little formal education. He told me he learned that shaded script from a calling-card writer in a carnival. He likes showy things and considers himself an elegant dresser. His shoes might have no soles, but the uppers would be shined, and probably yellow."

12

I got the general idea as I opened the letter. The cheap stationery bore the imprint of a Los Angeles hotel I had never heard of. The careful, shaded handwriting, in violet ink, filled the page and came out evenly at the bottom. I figured it had been recopied several times.

Sweetie:
   You will no dobt be suprized to here from me agin and know I am back in the Big Town. I had a war job in L.A. and did alright. I herd you on the radio and you are swell. You dont owe me nothing and woulden go for that old times sake routine and I woulden ask but it's not for me I'm asking. We had a kid and that makes us still pardners and thats why I have to see you and talk to you on account of her. Meet me Fri. aft. five oclock in the Comodore lobby.

Your
Eddie

I folded the page, returned it to the envelope. Dawn moved uneasily in her chair. I said, "I seem to catch an overtone of blackmail."

"I didn't know what it was, or what he wanted. I didn't answer it. I put in a wretched week waiting for him to turn up at the studio or the apartment. Without the extension number, it's practically impossible to call me at the studio, and I have an unlisted number at home, but I was afraid to answer the phone. Eddie always seemed to know—how to reach me."

"Did he show?"

"No word, no letters. Nothing. I began to breathe easily. Then—last Friday—something happened. I know it sounds crazy. But . . . a little girl was kidnaped. You must have read about it. Little Bette Alexander."

I'd read about it. Read every detail. Followed that case as if I'd been hired for it. All my life, I followed every big crime as if it were my own particular problem. Dad taught me that. He wanted a son who would grow up to make his mark on the Force. I was a girl, but he treated me as a boy . . . almost. Every big murder, every major crime—as long as it wasn't too bad—he'd tell me all the details and how he'd solve it if he were a detective instead of a cop.

So I knew about Bette Alexander. How she disappeared from her family's estate on Long Island on Friday afternoon. How the police had received only one note from the kidnapers and were still waiting for that bid for final contact.

Dawn Ferris sat very straight in her chair. "Miss Gallagher, I can't be sure, but—Bette Alexander may be my little girl."

This honey-haired woman, who called herself Dawn Ferris, paced the floor of my office as she talked, spilling out the story of this notion that had become an obsession in her mind. Now I could relax; she was really getting to the core of her visit.

"I didn't actually believe it at first," she said. "It was only . . . something familiar about the little girl's picture. Then as I kept looking at the picture in the paper, it began to seem much more real—more certain. The face—the features—were so familiar. I got out an old picture of Eddie, the earliest one I had, and compared them. They could have been brother and sister. As if that weren't enough, the paper gave Bette Alexander's

14

birthday, Miss Gallagher. It was the birthday of my little girl. Do you see? I wasn't crazy. I wasn't dreaming. Can you understand? This *was* my little girl."

She caught hold of herself. "I wasn't deliberately trying to believe it. I didn't want to believe it. But this girl was gone—nobody knew where. She might be murdered. I've walked like this"—she indicated her path through my office with a sweep of her hand—"for three nights. I've been trying to talk myself out of it, but I can't. It's too much . . . too perfect for coincidence. It couldn't . . ."

"Dawn," I used her first name deliberately, "sit down. You can't let it beat you . . . even if you're right. And in spite of all you say, the chances are a thousand to one you're wrong."

She sat down slowly, crossed her legs, lighted another cigarette. Then she opened that big purse, drew out a newspaper clipping and a small glossy photograph. "Look at these."

The clipping I'd seen before. It showed a reproduction of a painting of Bette Alexander, done by John Bartley Crane, the society artist. A tilt-nosed, freckle-faced girl with peaked eyebrows and a firm little chin, a gamin in an Abercrombie and Fitch riding habit.

Then I looked at the photograph and it looked right back at me, bold and impudent. A slim young fellow in a dark coat, ice-cream pants, and a bow tie, with a skimmer tucked under his arm. A young fellow with a tip-tilt nose, winged brows, and a look in his eyes Dad would have called devil-may-care. A pouty, buttonhole mouth and a weak chin robbed the eyes of their promise, but the face was still unusual.

15

I moved the photograph and clipping close together for comparison. The man and girl looked exactly alike except that the girl's mouth had wide, generous, well-formed lips. It could have been Dawn Ferris's mouth and chin.

Dawn was leaning over the desk.

"You see?" She was almost childishly eager for confirmation. "It can't be coincidence."

"I've known of more extraordinary coincidences," I stalled. "You've lived with this bottled up inside you for days. When the kidnap story broke, your mind began to make things fit. You could be right. But you aren't really thinking in terms of facts. . . ."

Patsy, in spite of her flightiness, always keeps files of major cases. I pressed the buzzer and asked for the folder on the Alexander case. It wasn't much—only newspaper clippings. Yet they made it simple, on the surface at least, to tear Dawn's theories to shreds.

"Bette Alexander is not an adopted child," I told her. "Theodore Alexander, the father, left his entire fortune in trust for that youngster when he died six months ago. The mother only gets an income. Would a man leave all that to an adopted child and not mention in his will that she was adopted? Of course, adopted children share equally with what the law calls issue, but this isn't a question of equality. Bette Alexander inherited the works."

Dawn didn't answer. She kept looking at me as though she realized fully this was only what it said in the paper—it made no difference in her mind.

"Further," I persisted, "you tell me that your child's

adoption was carried out in complete secrecy. If that is so, how could Eddie know where she was?"

She shrugged. "How did Eddie ever find out anything?"

A shaft of sunlight fell across the Benton landscape. It was such a peaceful scene, so remote from the inner turmoil of this woman. A mere glance fortified me, reduced the risk of emotional contagion.

I began making notes on my scratch pad, things she had mentioned. Names. "This Dr. Wurber," I said. "Have you contacted him since that time?"

"He still has that house in the Sixties, but apparently isn't there very often. I called several times. He has a service to take messages. That girl asked if I wanted an appointment, but I couldn't bring myself to make one. You see, I couldn't be sure . . ."

"And you knew he wouldn't tell you, even if you were right," I finished. "Besides, you didn't want him to know who you are now." She nodded bleakly and I went on. "How about Eddie? Any idea how to reach him? How about cronies in New York? Or former haunts?"

"I don't know where he stayed. I don't think he's got any cronies. He isn't the type who keeps friends."

I tossed my pencil down. "This isn't our kind of case, Miss Ferris. The FBI and the police are working on the Alexander investigation. Go to them. If your hunch is right, you should go to them."

"I can't and you know it," she shot at me. "It means ruining everything on a chance. I don't want to wreck my life—twice."

Her hands tightened on her purse and for a moment

I thought she was going to cry. I concentrated on those two pictures on the desk. Tears baffle me. I don't cry over important things—only movies and books—so I can't judge the emotion fairly. But after that first moment's hesitation, instead of crumpling, Dawn sprang to her feet, releasing a soft wave of perfume and a flash of the fight that brought her from burlesque performer to finished actress in ten years.

Suddenly—surprisingly—I found myself liking her. The look of determination on her face was interesting. The kind of look you would have expected on the face of Ann Preston, Woman Physician. Maybe phony, put on like her lipstick, but she was carrying the thing off. You had to admire her for it. I was about to say I'd consider handling the case, but she was ahead of me.

"I'm not asking you to investigate the kidnaping, but your business, Miss Gallagher, as I understand it, is tracing missing persons, people not involved with the law."

"More or less," I agreed airily, "that's how I make a living."

"Then I want to engage your services to try to locate for me the baby girl born to Edward and Ethel Wells on May fifth, 1933."

"And just incidentally," I added, "I might become involved in the Alexander kidnaping?"

"All I want," she said slowly, "is for you to tell me—prove to me—that I'm wrong. I want to know that Bette Alexander is not my child. I want to know just that much."

She laid her hand flat on the desk, then moved it slowly. Two crisp thousand-dollar bills looked up at me.

My first astonished reflection was that such big bills didn't get around enough to be worn limp. I got my breath and said, "It's a bit over my usual fee."

She smiled. "It's not a usual case. Will you hunt for her?"

"I'd hunt elephants," I said, picking up the bills, "for the proper fee."

Dawn sat down again on the edge of the chair, took a lipstick and large compact from her purse, and drew on a fresh mouth. She glanced up at my words with a touch of triumph. "It's such a relief to know someone else is with me on this. You can't imagine what it's been like."

"You can't imagine how we may get involved," I said, making out the forms for her signature. "Suppose Eddie is in this—even helped engineer it? Would you be willing . . ."

"If that's the case," she spoke slowly, as she signed the agreement, "we'll—find some way to handle it."

She said it curiously, as though she already had a plan. She was putting the lipstick and compact in her purse. It was only an instant that the big bag was tipped toward me. Yet I spotted the glittering object inside. She pulled the zipper closed. "Then I'll hear from you, Miss Gallagher?"

"Give me a couple of days," I said.

She moved toward the door with buoyant professional grace. Watching her, I wondered why Dawn Ferris carried a nickel-plated automatic in her purse.

$2.$ I BROKE a date for dinner that evening. I had too much on my mind for company. I dined alone at a place on Central Park South, near my apartment.

Louis, my favorite waiter, assured me everything was to my liking, and I took his word for it. For once I wasn't paying attention to food. I was too busy considering the facts I'd gathered on Eddie Wells.

After Dawn left, Patsy and I set to work to earn those two lovely green bills. Digging up information fast isn't easy, but I know a couple of places specializing in information on theatrical people. I shot Patsy over to those agencies.

By midafternoon she had an envelope of faded press clippings and cracked publicity pictures, covering the vaudeville days of Eddie Wells. There were also pictures of his partner, Ethel Wells, in buckety hats and knee-high dresses that would have set the present Dawn Ferris's teeth on edge.

Our own master files turned up more recent leads. There were several inquiries on Eddie Wells, variously known as Ed Welsh and Ned Wills. These were warning sheets from Western agencies who were looking for him. We wired for details.

I didn't expect much from these inquiries. They were

after him for bad debts. For my money, it's a waste of time to trace men like Eddie for debts. They're dead beats and strictly uncollectible. But they're easy people to trail.

I checked with the Bureau of Vital Statistics. There was no record of a child born to Edward and Ethel Wells on May 5, 1933. But there was a birth certificate recorded on that day for Elizabeth Anne, daughter of Theodore and Sylvia Alexander. I asked for a photostat.

I reread news stories on the kidnaping. On Friday afternoon Bette Alexander had stepped from the station wagon of the exclusive Purvence School, waved to her friends, and run through the gates of the family's palatial home near Huntington, Long Island. She was not seen again. A thin, rather plain child, she was tall for her fourteen years, an excellent swimmer, and a fine horsewoman. An accident was suspected until the ransom note was received on Saturday night. Then the FBI joined the Suffolk County police in the hunt.

There were interviews with Bette's mother, Sylvia Alexander, a handsome blonde of about forty, and with M. E. Baxter, the Alexander family lawyer and an executor of the estate. Also with John Bartley Crane, society artist, specializing in portraits of children, whose recent painting of Bette had been so widely used.

I called up a few people I knew. One of Dad's old pals, a former Suffolk County detective, now working on the Alexander case, also a *News* reporter who had a by-line story on it. I kept my questions very casual, but from what I gathered in talking to them, there wasn't the slightest indication that Bette was the adopted daughter of Sylvia and Theodore Alexander. Besides.

there was also that matter of the estate I'd mentioned to Dawn. Would a man leave his entire fortune to an adopted child without some mention of that legal angle?

Very thoughtfully I left the restaurant and walked out into the soft March evening. Spring was early, but early or late, it irritated me. Spring always does. It seems to affect a weak and defenseless appeal, like a fragile female in white. I like autumn. Autumn is mature and strong and able to take care of itself.

But spring was with me that night, fuzzing everything into gentle curves, giving the bare trees a slightly pregnant look. There was a fragrance from the park that defied the aggressive fumes of carbon monoxide and incineration. There was rain in the air, and the low clouds were luminous from the lights of midtown Manhattan. I belted my all-weather coat, pulled the brim of my felt hat forward, and set out toward Central Park West. I like to walk in the rain. And besides, I wanted to look at a house in the West Sixties.

The address was in that narrow wedge of streets formed by Broadway and the west boundary of the Park. There was a large apartment house at the corner where I turned left toward Broadway. Behind the elegant frontage facing the Park, the street seemed to crumble. In the shadow of fine buildings and lofty towers, old brownstone houses huddled in shabby embarrassment.

Here spring was defeated. Moldy cellars, stale beer, and furnished-room cookery won out. The street lights were far-spaced and dim. The lights from the houses added only furtive bleakness. I walked faster, stumbled against a refuse can midway from the curb. A radio somewhere blared with studio laughter. A child cried.

A couple walked past me, arguing—a young couple full of bitterness. Ethel and Eddie might have been like that.

Two doors from the next corner I spotted the house, primly respectable among its slatternly neighbors. The doorknob shone. The long front windows gleamed against chastely drawn drapes. There was no light visible. A tiny name plate in metal gleamed against the stone. Dr. Wurber. No initials, no Christian name, just the identification. Dr. Wurber.

I mounted the high stone steps and pressed the bell. I heard it jangle through the house. I pressed a second time, more persistent than hopeful. The echo had an empty sound.

"Well, now, and what do you want?"

The sudden gruff voice so startled me I almost went over backward. He was standing in the small areaway at the side of the steps where a door led into the basement. Though he was half lost in the shadows, I could make out dimly the scowling face of a thickset, white-haired man in shirt sleeves and suspenders.

"Who is it you're after?" he asked, with a stubborn hostility.

I came down the steps quickly. I smiled and said gently, "You startled me. Didn't know where the voice came from. I wanted to see Dr. Wurber."

"Not in. Won't be in."

"You're sure?" I leaned against the iron rail surrounding the areaway. The old man, only a few feet from me now, stared nearsightedly.

"Did you—have an appointment, ma'am?" His tone softened.

"I thought I did," I said breathlessly. "I came so far . . ."

The myopic eyes peered with embarrassing directness in the general area of my waist. I was thankful for the bunchy coat.

"Did you have an appointment for this night?" he persisted.

"It's—April twenty-fifth, isn't it?"

"It is that," he said, edging out of the enclosure as he fumbled in his pants pocket. "Doctor's a great hand for comin' unbeknownst to me. Sometimes meetin' his patients right here on the step. Would you be early now?"

"I might. Is it eight-thirty?"

" 'Tisn't that yet," he said in obvious relief, and went before me up the steps. "I shouldn't be lettin' you in, but the night's damp an' in your condition . . ."

He unlocked the front door, switched on the lights, and led me into the big living room. I took a bill from the wallet in my pocket, pressed it into the gnarled hand.

"You've been so kind," I murmured.

He beamed under thatched brows. "Nothin' at all, ma'am. My wife went through it eleven times an' I always say if you stay out of the night air . . ."

I sat in a large leather chair near the double doors, and picked up a magazine as the old fellow left. I didn't move until I heard him go down the outer steps and close the basement door.

Luck, I decided, was riding with me. I couldn't be sure there were any fourteen-year-old files here, but it was too good a possibility to pass. The answer to the whole thing—whether or not Dawn Ferris's child and Bette Alexander were the same person—might be tucked away in some neat corner in this office.

I waited until everything was quiet. No sound at all if you counted out the pounding of my own heart. But the janitor might be somewhere below, listening. I kicked off my pumps, moved cautiously, in stockinged feet. The carpet pricked through my nylons as I crossed the room. A gloomy room, long, narrow, and high-ceil-inged; the windows, only at the front, were shrouded in long, beige draperies. There was a scattering of heavy dark furniture and an aura reminiscent of the convent infirmary, a mixture of closed rooms and medications.

I reached the dark oak doors with the frosted glass paneling that formed the office partition. Except for my shoes, I was still dressed for the street, including gloves. I took a firm grip on the knob and turned gently. The door opened.

The light from the one lamp behind me revealed only shadow on the waxed linoleum floor. I reached out for the wall switch, found a panel with several but-tons, pressed one.

Instantly I was bathed in glaring white light, sudden as a scream. I shut it off quickly, but the picture of the room was fixed in my mind, like a scene viewed by light-ning. I could have diagramed the desk, chairs, files, and bookcases, the two long windows at the rear with shades drawn level with the sills. There was no evidence of surgical equipment. This must be an office and con-sulting room.

In the far corner beyond the desk was a group of fil-ing cabinets, on which stood a gooseneck lamp. Not trusting the light buttons, I followed the line of the wall, my cold feet in sweat-damp stockings sliding on the waxed floor. The light from the living room guided me past major hazards. Carefully I reached the lamp, tipped the shade low, and turned the switch. For once I was happy to see the dim yellow gleam of a twenty-five-watt bulb.

Before me were two tiers of green metal filing cabinets. I pulled gently at the top drawer. The doctor evidently wasn't worried about intruders. The drawer slid open easily. It was filled with eight-by-five folder-type cards, designed for the history of the patient and his correspondence.

Only there was no correspondence. The folder sections were empty. The cards, however, were all filled out in the same neat square handwriting. It was the second bit of unusual penmanship I'd seen that day. But this was the extreme opposite of Eddie Wells's florid, show-card hand. This script recalled the writing on library cards when I was a kid. Every card in every drawer was written in that same style. Hundreds of them, and every entry made by the same person.

I squatted on my heels to reach the W's in the bottom drawer and flipped through the carefully filed cards. Dr. Wurber had a passion for organization. He could give Patsy lessons in filing. Welch—Weller—Wells . . .

My hand shook as I drew out the large card. The writing danced before my eyes. I held the card closer to the dim light. Wells, Norma . . . I could almost taste my disappointment. Quickly I went back to the file. The next card was Wellward. I put it back slowly.

Were these really case histories? If so, how far back

did they date? I pulled out the record of Norma Wells again. It was dated January 1942, but there was no street address or telephone number on the lines provided for that information. The many other entries looked like algebra problems, with letters and numbers together. Obviously the thing was in code.

I looked at several others. All the same. Names only and one date. All other entries coded. I ran through other cards in the W's, noting dates. They went back to 1928. If Ethel Wells had ever been here, there should be a card.

Putting the file in order, I closed the drawer. These might be records of foster mothers. If Dr. Wurber delivered Ethel Wells's child, he would have placed her for adoption. And if that child was now known as Bette Alexander . . . I started to rise but my legs were stiff from the cramped position. I stretched up slowly. Slowly, too, I was aware of a change.

The house was no longer still. Not that there was any definite noise. Simply that the place was no longer empty. Without turning, I realized there was someone close. Someone behind me, in the doorway. It could be the Irish janitor, but I knew it wasn't. I continued upward by slow motion to a standing position. My own breathing seemed to stop.

"I would stay right there, if I were you."

The voice was querulous but authoritative, as if the words were reinforced with steel—or lead. I stood rigid, staring at the gracefully curving gooseneck lamp.

"I am surprised," the voice went on, in an injured tone, "that he would resort to such methods. Does he think I'm a fool?"

There was obviously no answer to that, so early in our acquaintance. But who did he think I was?

"Face me!"

I moved very slowly, trying to frame a good out. It was only seconds. Then I confronted a short, plump, middle-aged man. He was totally bald and his round face hairless except for thick sandy eyebrows, unexpected as parsley on a custard. His tan gabardine suit was smartly tailored, his linen custom made, his surprisingly small narrow shoes gleaming. In his small fat hand he held a small square gun. In that peculiar way my mind works, the hand reminded me of the writing on those cards.

If my initial survey was thorough, it was also quick. He, in turn, looked me over with irritating deliberation from my Knox hat to my shoeless feet.

"You are lovely," he said finally. "He told me you were but I didn't believe it. I expected something younger and cheaper. The floozy type. What does he have to offer a girl like you?" He was moving around me. "Take off your hat."

I took it off. He moved closer, teetering like an unsure ballet dancer. I had an unpleasant feeling that he was going to touch my hair. I didn't like those lard-white hands. I didn't like him. If only I could find out who I was supposed to be . . .

"A brunette on the auburn side. I thought you were more of a redhead," he said. "Intelligent, too. Much too intelligent to get involved with a down-at-heel punk like Eddie Wells."

I gave an involuntary start. Noting it, his lips parted in an unpleasant variation of a smile.

"You see I did know you, Cora. Eddie told me about you when I went to see him in that hole—last Thursday." He made a disgusted sound in his throat. "He didn't mention that he would send you to search my office."

For a moment I felt dizzy. Eddie Wells . . . Cora . . . Eddie's girl friend, obviously. They somehow were linked with this man, and as recently as last Thursday, the day before the kidnaping. I was on the track of what I was seeking, but where it might eventually lead I didn't know.

"Since we recognize each other, Dr. Wurber," I said, "you can put the gun down. I am not armed."

He studied me from under those eyebrows, decided to accept my statement, dropped the gun into his outer coat pocket, waved his hand to the chair beside his desk.

"Sit down, Cora."

I obeyed almost gratefully. He pressed the proper button on the panel and soft wall lights went on. Then very deliberately he sat in his big chair, just around the edge of the desk from me. Silently he lined his pencil, pen, and paper cutter on the blotter before him. I half expected him to produce one of those big cards.

"You are a very foolish girl," he said, in that thin whine. "I could have you arrested for gaining entry under false pretenses."

That was a bluff. My confidence mounted faintly from zero. I made my eyes wide.

"I hope you wouldn't do that, Dr. Wurber. Eddie would be mad."

"I don't see why you should mind what he thinks." His eyes were still on their sight-seeing tour. I crossed my knees, deliberately, smiling apologetically as I glanced from him to my shoeless foot. His eyes beat mine by seconds. I drew my feet together demurely under the chair. The guy gave me the creeps.

"I don't see why you should mind at all," he repeated impatiently. "About him, I mean."

"Perhaps I'm fond of him."

Wurber made an unpleasant chortling sound. "What women see in him . . ."

"I suppose girls want to mother him," I said softly.

"Well, I want no part of him. All my years in New York—not a word against me—and now this!"

"You mean last week—or tonight?"

His pale eyes peered from under those brows like clams in a cave. "Tonight?"

"That wasn't like you thought—like it looked."

"No?"

"I was curious, that's all. I didn't want that nice janitor to hear me, so I took off my shoes. I hope you won't tell Eddie."

"My dear young lady, I never expect to speak to him again on any subject. I thought I made that clear to him."

"He said . . ."

"He said . . . he said . . ." Wurber parroted. "Whatever he said, I believe none of it."

He pulled out a faintly scented handkerchief, mopped his brow. I glanced down at my gloved hands, folded in my lap, and figured my chances. Dad always said play your cards as though you held a royal flush. The next play in this game was a hazard.

"Eddie didn't send me here," I began, and the tremor in my voice was genuine. "I came because I thought you . . . were his friend."

He gave an impatient grunt. I kept on, without looking at him, feeling the thin mounting tension I'd known as a little girl when I made up stories to tell Grandma. "Eddie's hurt."

"You mean—Eddie has taken offense—at me?" Wurber was getting cute.

"I mean—he's injured. Shot."

"Shot!" Wurber squeaked. "By whom? How?"

"It was an accident." My nervousness was a helpful prop to the act. "He slammed the drawer, the gun was in there, went off. The bullet grazed him."

Wurber obviously didn't believe my account of the accident. "You should have called an ambulance if he's badly hurt."

"I would have, but to get an ambulance from a city hospital you have to call the police first. Even private hospitals—and most doctors—report an accident with firearms. Don't they?"

The doctor ignored the question, asked another with icy annoyance. "And Eddie doesn't want to see the police?"

"You know that."

"Where is he?" Wurber demanded irritably.

"In . . . that hole, as you called it."

"Curse the day I ever saw the man," Wurber muttered. "He's always brought trouble."

"But you must come," I persisted. "You couldn't let him die. That would bring the police, too."

I didn't look at him. I kept my eyes lowered, for the demure effect, the helpless, spring expression. "You will come?"

"I am still a doctor," he said crossly, "even though—at times—I think it would be better if some people were to die."

A soft veil of rain enveloped the street when we came out. An impressive car with a New Jersey license was parked a few doors away. I was sure it belonged to Wurber, but he ignored it and headed toward Broadway. At the corner, in front of a dingy, eighth-rate hotel, we picked up a cab. I popped into it, my hand on the opposite door handle, just in case.

The cabby was looking at him. Wurber hesitated, glanced at me. My hand tightened on the door handle. My expression, I hoped, was perfectly blank. Wurber gave a number on Third Avenue, got in, and sat beside me, close. I released the door handle.

The driver looked around. "Is that in the Seventies?"

"Near Ninetieth Street," I said automatically. I'd been dunning a man only a few numbers away.

Dr. Wurber nodded. His bushy eyebrows close together under the brim of his hat gave him a totally different appearance. With him, a hat was a disguise. He settled back, his knees spread, touching mine.

I sat in rigid silence, my mind ticking faster than the meter as we crossed 72nd Street and entered the Park. The silent rain misted the lights and the windshield, filled the air with fragrance. I tried to relax, get an easier hold on myself, but my nerves wouldn't unbend.

What I needed was a good plan, and how could you

plan when you didn't know what came next? This could be a trap in reverse. Wurber might be leading me into one of his own. I had to take that chance.

The cab wound skillfully through the maze of drives, the tires singing on the wet road. The buildings along Central Park South gleamed like a fairy city through the rose-gray mist. I thought of the nice safe restaurant where I had dinner and of my apartment, around the corner from it. Surely nothing serious could happen this close to home. Dr. Wurber's elbow brushed mine and I started.

"Cigarette?"

I took one, accepted his light, couldn't avoid his fat little finger lingering against mine. My skin crawled. After all his dealings with women over the years, I wondered he ever wanted to see or touch another one; but he obviously did.

The cab crossed Fifth Avenue, headed east, then took Park Avenue, north. It was such a very little way now. I tried to empty my mind. This was no time for crossing bridges, coming or going. I had connected Dr. Wurber with Eddie Wells. If he took me to Eddie Wells, he might take me indirectly to Eddie Wells's child.

The cab turned under the elevated into Third Avenue. I noted the number on the first store. The address Dr. Wurber gave was in the middle of the short block. It was a rag-tag section, with cheap flats and rooming houses over small stores, the entrances to the dwellings wedged between the shops.

We stopped. Wurber paid the driver and we crossed the wet sidewalk, Wurber clutching his black bag and picking his way in those small pointed shoes. I strode

33

into the dingy entrance as though I knew where I was going. There were some battered mailboxes in the dirty wall of the vestibule, bells with indecipherable name plates. The door opened when a man walked out. I caught the door and Wurber and I walked in.

The hall smelled of bad plumbing, cooked cabbage, and everlasting darkness. I hung back, let Wurber go before me up the creaking, grease-slippery stairs. A girl of about fifteen ran past us down the stairs, her child mouth heavy with make-up, her cheap red sling pumps clattering. I shuddered. Certainly I've seen poverty, and drab little girls trying to be beautiful. But there was something about this place that was worse than poor, worse than dirty. It had an almost melodramatic air of evil, like a scene in a movie. A dingy, damp, friendless place.

Dr. Wurber, panting, turned at the third-floor landing. I followed him through the narrow hall, lighted by a single feeble bulb. He stopped before a door. So did I.

"Well, let us in," he said impatiently. I put out my hand before I realized what he meant.

"I . . . I don't have a key." Still holding the knob, I knocked with my free hand. There was no answer. I knocked again. Dr. Wurber was fuming.

"Coming out . . . leaving this man . . . anybody could have walked in."

I turned the knob. The door was unlocked. Cool air blew across my face as I pushed the door open. I realized a window was raised. I reached for the wall switch as a train roared by, shaking the building like an earthquake. In the passing glare, I glimpsed the line of the light cord in the middle of the room. I moved quickly and pulled on the light.

With my hand still on the greasy, fly-specked cord, I surveyed the dingy kitchen-sitting room. Empty beer bottles and crusts from sandwiches littered the deal table. A fact-detective magazine lay on a chair near the window.

Behind me Wurber was saying, "Where is he? What have . . ."

There was a door ajar, leading into another room. I said, "In there. That's where he was."

There are some things you know. Some things you know without ever realizing how the meaning came to you. But this was not one of those occasions. I had no premonition as Wurber pushed open the door. I was on his heels as he stopped, gasped, muttered oaths as he found the pull cord for the light. Then he stepped aside.

Lying on that rumpled, unmade bed, still in trousers and shirt, was Eddie Wells. No mistaking the face, the upturned nose, the winged brows, the petulant mouth. Nor was there any mistaking the hideous hole in his forehead, the dark smear of blood across the upper half of his face, the crimson splotches on his shirt.

Dr. Wurber was staring at me. Accusation—ghastly clear—burned in those pale eyes.

I'd said Eddie was shot. That was what I told Wurber—to bring him here. And I'd been right. That was the fantastic fact I had to face now.

Eddie had been shot. He was dead.

3.

I HAD seen death neatly dressed in a coffin, but never like this, raw and rude, with staring eyes. Eddie Wells had met death literally face to face. Obviously he had been backed into the dirty cluttered bedroom at gunpoint and shot. There had been no struggle. His hair was neatly combed. The crease still marked his trousers.

Dr. Wurber, his breath an audible rattle, bent with dainty gestures over the bed. "Dead for hours," he murmured, as he straightened up, his eyes glassy as marbles, sweat visible on the slick skin. He teetered toward me on those little feet.

"Eddie's injured!" His natural falsetto climbed an octave in satirical mimicry. "He's been shot. That's what you said."

"But . . ." I stammered in panic. "I didn't realize— how badly . . ."

"Stop lying," he squealed. "You said he was wounded. He was dead then. He died instantly."

"I didn't kill him," I said, grabbing at truth. The very honest denial gave me courage. "You have to understand that, now, this instant. This is only between you and me. Cards-on-the-table stuff. I didn't kill him."

Wurber looked at the body again, a cold, professional

look. Then slowly he turned and faced me. "Who are you?"

"You know who I am."

"No. You're not Eddie's girl. You had some reason for getting me here, for dragging me into this. You had a reason."

He picked up his case, bustled into the wretched living room.

"What are you going to do now?" I asked, trying to hold that new steadiness.

"I'm getting out. Understand? He's your business if you are Cora, and you can take care of it. I never saw you in my life."

I turned out the lights automatically, like a housekeeper finished with the cleaning. As I put out the living-room light, another El train rushed by, rattling dishes and pans on the stove. A man could be machine-gunned with that racket going on and nobody would ever hear.

Wurber said, "You open the door. You're wearing gloves."

I obeyed him. Instantly he pushed past me, rushing through the narrow hall and down the stairs. I hurried after him, grabbed his arm.

"Don't run," I cautioned, as a door opened on the first floor. With a sigh like a pneumatic brake the little doctor slowed down, took each step with exaggerated deliberation. A large woman in a soiled house dress and a shoulder-length bob of matted gray hair came to the foot of the stairs. Looking up at us, with large dark eyes, she was rather handsome, or would have been if she were well groomed, or even scrubbed.

"You the doctor?" she asked Wurber, with a foreign accent. He nodded. "That poor Mr. Wells . . ." Wurber's fat shoulders quivered. She went on sympathetically, "Such a nice guy. Real cute, huh? How is he?"

"He's resting," Wurber squeaked. "There's nothing more I can do for him."

"Ahhh! I go in after while. Maybe the blonde lady is up there? She come back?"

"The blonde lady?" I broke in.

"She go for the doctor." It was half statement, half question.

"Oh, yes, that one. She isn't here right now."

"Such a beautiful lady." The big woman smiled, revealing two missing teeth. "Such beautiful ladies he knows."

I kept moving slowly, smiling, too, as I passed the landlady. Wurber, ahead of me, had bolted out to the street. I followed leisurely, aware that she was still watching us.

The rain had stopped but the streets were wet and glistening. We hadn't been in there more than ten minutes.

"I'll go uptown," Wurber said. "You go some other way."

He took off with a flying leap. I stood, watched him flag down a cab at the next corner. I was definitely rocky. I had to take it easy, get everything under control before I saw people or they saw me. I dug out a cigarette, took a deep drag. I glanced at my watch. Ten-ten. Deliberately I turned and walked south toward the lights at 86th Street.

A police radio car came along the curb, parked. I wanted to run but I didn't. I moved mechanically, my eyes fixed on those lights, some five blocks away. The cop in the car was making out a report. The police didn't know about Eddie, yet.

With each measured step, I knew I should turn back, show the police my credentials, tell them there was a dead man in the third-floor front flat, two doors down. But I wasn't ready. I wanted to think, to figure the angles. For instance, the blonde who went for the doctor. Dawn Ferris was a blonde. . . .

I crossed the next street. It was a dark block. A train roared overhead. In the silence that followed, I heard footsteps, heavy and slightly uneven. I slackened my pace. So did the footsteps. I didn't like it. Neither did my nerves. Chills crawled on the back of my neck, while dark thoughts slid through my mind.

Punks gathered strange companions in a lifetime of petit larceny. Somebody thought it necessary to kill Eddie Wells. That somebody might have been watching when Wurber and I entered the building, and when we came out. My ears strained with listening. There was no sound but those footsteps measured to mine.

In the middle of the block there was a dimly lit delicatessen store. I stopped before the window, stared at a toothy cardboard blonde, holding out a glass of beer. With a minimum of motion I cast a side glance up the street. There was no one in sight.

I really turned and looked then. Not a soul between me and the house in the next block where Eddie lay. I drew a deep breath, started on. I was just beyond the

39

friendly lights of the store when the steps resumed. Heavy . . . light . . . heavy. It could be a cop but they don't have lame cops.

The blocks are short. I was near the corner. I walked faster. The steps speeded effortlessly as though, limping or not, they were easily geared to a change of pace. The next block was bright—a drugstore, a bar. My foot touched the curb. The traffic light changed. A stream of westbound traffic rolled slowly by. The steps had not stopped. They were on my heels.

Behind a limousine and a truck came a cab. I darted out toward it, saw two heads close together in the back before I caught the driver's negative signal. Reluctantly I returned to the curb. Those steps were louder and louder and then they stopped. He was standing too close to me, too close for strangers on a street corner.

I glanced down, saw the gray trousers, the edge of the blue raincoat. The coat moved nearer. The man was tall, very tall; the top of my head was level with his shoulder. I couldn't plunge ahead into that swishing traffic. I might have turned east at that corner, but I seemed frozen to the sidewalk as the man's sleeve brushed my cheek. Then he spoke, his words low and distinct, the tone commanding.

"I must talk to you," he said, "about your recent call —on a corpse."

4. I LOOKED up slowly. I don't know what I expected to see, but it was not what I saw. The man was a young thirty, and handsome in a highbred, sensitive way. Even his battered hat had an air of distinction, striking a note of intention rather than necessity. I didn't miss the look of surprise in his eyes either. It restored my breath and a small degree of my confidence. I tried to make the confidence look big.

"Who are you?" I asked bluntly.

"I was about to put the same question. Was Eddie Wells sending out invitations this evening?"

So he, too, had come to see Eddie. That clinched it for me. I said, "Shall we talk this over?"

"We can take a cab to my apartment," he suggested.

"We can walk to Dario's bar, two blocks from here," I countered flatly. Dario's was the one good place in that neighborhood, and Mike Nash was barman there. I wanted one friend on the premises.

He smiled faintly and nodded. I turned west with the man beside me, which was less nerve-racking than having him behind me, but tension walked with us, present as a third person. We moved rapidly. His limp was due to a rigid ankle, but it didn't cut down his swift stride. I kept right up with him, but fast as our feet moved my mind was far ahead.

How did he figure in this? He definitely wasn't the type I expected Eddie Wells to know. What did he mean by invitation? In the taut silence I tried to frame questions, but they didn't frame easily. We turned at Lexington Avenue; two more blocks, another turn, and Dario's window with its ribbon of neon light beckoned. We went down the three steps quickly.

Dario's is like a thousand such bars in Manhattan, a small basement room that was once a speak-easy. It was quiet as a public library, with a few people at the bar, another half dozen scattered at the round tables in the rear. Mike Nash, behind the bar, lifted a hand in greeting as I walked to the back, chose a table in the far corner.

I sank down into the comfortable old chair. The man took off his hat and coat. His gray tweed suit was definitely not new but expensive and had the look of English tailoring. His dark hair was unruly and he pushed it back with a mowing gesture. As he raised his arm I caught the dark glint of a dried stain on the edge of his gray coat sleeve . . . a slick hard line of stain, that might have been brown, might have been dark red.

I kept my eyes moving as he sat down, drew his chair to the side, surveyed the room. "No juke?" he asked.

"Do you miss it?"

"I'm very grateful," he said. Mike personally came for our order. He was always interested in my men, but this time I made a business of lighting a cigarette to avoid an introduction. The man ordered bourbon and soda, and I nodded in agreement.

"Got some of your favorite Scotch, Gale," Mike whispered, but I smiled, shook my head.

"You seem to be known around here—Gale," the man said when Mike went away.

"Mike and I went to P. S. Sixty-three together. But I'm well known in a lot of places." I took my wallet from my pocket, flipped it open to my identification. He raised one eyebrow, grinned. It made him look younger.

"How do you do, Miss Gallagher?" he said, taking out his wallet, a bulky affair with many transparent sections for cards. He opened it to his driver's license. "Sorry the city doesn't furnish such impressive identifications for artists."

"Artist!" I read the name—John Bartley Crane, 1280 West 57th Street. "An artist . . . and practically neighbor. I live only a few blocks away."

I leaned back in the chair, relaxed. Of all the people I could have imagined, an artist was the most unlikely. I got one very deep breath before my mind did a double take. John Bartley Crane . . . who did portraits of children, who did the much-publicized picture of Bette Alexander.

The tension snapped back. Mike brought the drinks. I really needed mine. Crane seemed calm, and his eyes, measuring me, were cool and noncommittal. I was sure he spotted the exact moment when I connected him with the Alexander case.

"You mentioned an invitation, Mr. Crane. Do I understand Mr. Wells invited you around this evening?"

"He did. At least that was the name the man gave me on the telephone this afternoon. He insisted it was very urgent that I call on him."

"Couldn't he come to see you?"

"He had a rather dramatic excuse—said he was being watched. He further specified I come alone." Crane sipped his drink. "I explained that I was seeing a client off at La Guardia Field at seven. I could make it about eight. The flight was delayed, so it was after nine when I got back to Manhattan. I went directly there—and found a dead man."

I shivered, remembering the body of Eddie Wells. "I left at once," Crane continued with a wry grin. "It was nine-thirty. I crossed the street, stood in the doorway of a darkened store, and watched those windows in the third-floor front. Several persons went in the building, one man came out, then you and your friend arrived."

I said, "The Department could use you."

"I decided this evening I wouldn't like the work, especially when I saw that light go on in the third-floor front. Of course, one would feel differently with the Manhattan detective force in the supporting cast. I didn't know what my next move would be, when the light went off and you two appeared again. Your friend's departure settled it for me. I wondered if you had also received an invitation." Crane leaned his elbows on the table. "Who is Eddie Wells?"

"An ex-vaudeville hoofer and a dead beat . . . and I didn't mean that as a bad pun."

"Then that was Wells? That corpse?"

"You never saw him before?"

He shook his head. "Did you?"

"No, but I had descriptions. That was Eddie. But you didn't even know that. Why didn't you go to the police?"

"Why didn't you?" he countered.

"I didn't want to get involved," I said. "I . . . my business is collections and skip tracing. Murder is not my line."

I looked at him as I spoke, but he had a trick of retreating behind his eyes, raising a smile as a barricade. "I assure you, Miss Gallagher, murder is no specialty of mine, either. Do you ordinarily take a doctor with you to collect bills?"

"That was a . . . friend. It's a rough neighborhood."

"From my vantage point, it appeared that your friend abandoned you rather summarily. He at least could have called a cab for you."

That smile was still in Crane's eyes as he offered me a cigarette. I declined and watched in silence as he took one. The dark stain on the edge of his sleeve glittered ominously as he raised his hand. Could he be a killer, this man who made a career of painting little children? He didn't look like a murderer, but he didn't look like an artist, I reflected, if a man can look like his profession. He suggested a research chemist, or a doctor; though that wormy little Wurber didn't look like a doctor. I pulled my thoughts back to the more tangible problems in hand.

"Eddie Wells wanted to see you because you drew Bette Alexander's picture."

Crane looked at me through the flame as he lighted his cigarette, still looked at me as he snapped the lighter.

"And you wanted to see him for something more important than a bad debt. You knew there was trouble or you wouldn't have brought a doctor."

45

"I didn't know it," I said in half honesty.

"But you knew he had some connection with Bette Alexander."

"I don't know that either—I only know that you did. You made the one recent picture the family had of the child. You knew her."

"I do know her." He used the present tense with emphasis. "She's a wonderful youngster. I don't want anything to happen to her."

"Beyond what already has," I murmured. "But Eddie had information for you."

"He said he had, but I didn't really believe him."

"Just what did he say?"

Crane frowned. "It was rather garbled. He was talking from a pay station and whispering into the phone. He didn't come directly to the point, so I lost a minute before I realized what he was talking about. He said I was her friend."

"How could he be sure?" I was thinking of that letter to Dawn. "He didn't know you."

"No, but he knew about her coming to sit for her picture. But Bette never came in town alone. Either her mother, or Monty Baxter, the family lawyer, or Wilson, the Alexanders' houseman, drove her in. I don't see how he could have known."

Dawn had said Eddie could be amazingly efficient. Eddie always found out.

"What else did he say?"

"Just what I've told you. He gave me his name and address, and directions about coming alone. He sounded very nervous. He started to say something that sounded

46

like the word guardian, but then the operator cut in for another nickel. He hung up."

"A guardian? But Bette doesn't have a guardian."

"I puzzled over that, too. Her mother is her legal guardian. In fact, it was those bits—the business about knowing she came to my studio and this guardian stuff —that made me go there tonight. Otherwise I would have thought it one more crank." He grinned. "I've had several letters, implying that I kidnaped Bette and am holding her a prisoner in my *garret*." The tormenting grin spread. "You aren't the only one who doesn't trust artists, Miss Gallagher."

"Doesn't trust . . ." I began to protest, felt my face flame. "That's ridiculous. What difference would your profession make?"

"Oh, you wouldn't trust me on any count? Of course, I can see your point. I had opportunity to kill Eddie Wells, and perhaps the motive. If, as some of my correspondents charge, I had stolen Bette, Eddie played right into my hands. Men have died before for knowing too much."

"And women, too," I added. "You've made a very complete synopsis of my own thoughts, Mr. Crane. But why didn't you go to the police?"

"Wells said he himself was in danger and that I would endanger Bette's life if I went to the police. As the first statement has proven so obviously right, I hesitated . . ." He spun his glass in his long strong hands, stared at the miniature whirlpool. "Twice a week, during the month of February, Bette came to my studio. As you surmised, I got to know her. I worked longer than

47

usual on the picture, or rather on Bette as a subject. I made many sketches of her. She is definitely not photogenic. Her nose is too short, her jaw is too wide. She was all angles and shadows to a camera, but to me she was lovely."

His eyes were shining as though he were looking at her. "Bette is gay and friendly, gloriously curious. She's at that wonderful stage where one moment she is a tomboy, the next a sophisticated young lady. She brought a party dress for one sitting. For all of a half hour she was a dignified little subdeb; then, unmindful of the dress, she sprawled on the hearth, feet in the air, while she sketched and drank a coke." His voice rose suddenly. "Surely, no one could hurt her."

His own fierce burst of words startled him. He smiled apologetically, finished his drink. "I'm sorry," he said. "I haven't talked about it much. I don't do it very well."

He did it too well. His emotion was contagious. I was touched by his devotion to Bette. I wanted to tell him all I knew, try to piece it together. Why shouldn't I, when he was being so honest with me? I leaned forward, was about to speak, but at that moment there was a slight diversion.

A tall blonde girl, whom I had noticed before—she came in on our heels and stood at the bar—walked toward a small table against the wall. Crane's chair was at an angle and he had to move to let her pass. His glance followed her. Her figure was definitely eye-catching, and the slick red raincoat would have made her a cinch to shadow. Settled again in his chair, Crane signaled Mike for a repeat order. That momentary confusion acted as a brake on my runaway sympathies.

How did I know he was telling the truth? He was well educated and charming, but that's no proof of innocence. I'd gone soft for a minute—in the head as well as the heart. By the time Mike returned with the drinks, I had everything under control.

I let Crane talk about Bette, her talent of mimicry, her ability as an artist. "There isn't a stranger in the world to Bette, she likes everyone. Some of my young subjects imitate their snobbish elders, but not Bette. She's a child of the people."

"Was she adopted?" I tossed in casually.

"Adopted? What a peculiar question! Why do you ask? After all, the Alexanders are a very well-known family."

I ducked the question. "Oh, you knew the Alexanders before you did this picture of Bette?"

"Rather. My parents knew Bette's father, Theodore Alexander, very well. So well that I called him Uncle Ted. In fact, he was an old beau of my mother's."

"Bette's father—a beau of your mother?"

"That's right. He was thirty years older than his wife . . . didn't marry until he was well in his fifties."

"Then you also have known Sylvia Alexander for a long time?"

"Ever since her marriage. Bette was born while I was in college. After my parents died, I seldom saw Sylvia and Uncle Ted. It's only been this past year, since my return to my work—the Navy occupied me for a time—that I really got to know Sylvia. I wrote her when Uncle Ted died, then I saw her in town occasionally, and last Christmas she commissioned me to do Bette's picture."

So—just a friend of the family, I thought, as we finished our drinks, and Crane helped me with my coat. The interview had ended in a stalemate. There were moves I daren't make. Wasn't the same true of Crane?

"You've been very kind, Miss Gallagher," he was saying, "after I barged up to you so rudely. I don't know what I hoped to discover—perhaps that you were Wells's wife—or girl friend." .

I grinned. Twice in one evening I had been taken for that character. I was surprised that he didn't press me any further about my part in that visit, or question me about the doctor. Perhaps my story didn't appear as flimsy to him as it might to another detective. He said some more polite things as he paid the check.

On the way out, I stopped at the bar for a brief good night to Mike and a word about Libby, his wife, who was—as Mike discreetly put it—expecting. "Everything's fine with me," Mike said; then dropping his voice and cocking an eyebrow he asked, "On a case?" He had a disapproving admiration for my work, so at my assent he beamed with the air of a conspirator, and busily polished a glass as Crane approached. I knew I'd hear more about this the next time I dropped in.

Crane opened the door, then hesitated in the small entry. The rain was coming down heavily. "Will you share a cab with me now?" he asked. Actually I had no more real reason to trust him than I had an hour earlier, but at least I agreed to ride with him.

I waited in the entry as he went to hail a cab. Watching him walk with that swift uneven stride toward the corner, I thought there was something terribly attractive about the guy. I could see why Sylvia Alexander should go for him. I was wondering where that idea came from when the inner door opened and the blonde in the red raincoat came out.

I stepped back to let her pass. In the narrow space she was very close to me. I was reflecting how some girls, like this one, miss being beautiful by such a narrow margin, the absence of some intangible quality that makes for loveliness, that separates the illusively desirable from the cheaply attainable, when suddenly she stopped, glaring boldly at me from her few inches' advantage in height. I looked away quickly, embarrassed. Evidently I'd been staring at her without realizing it.

"Why don't you mind your own business?" she demanded in a harsh whisper. "Keep your hands off what don't belong to you. It'd be smart."

Her attack caught me completely off guard. This couldn't be due to a rude stare. Recovering my wits, I made a lunge after her, grabbed at the slick sleeve of her raincoat as she went up the steps to sidewalk level. I had a glove half on, so I didn't get a good grip. She spun quickly, threw me off.

I dashed up the steps after her, but she went streaking —a red flash through the rain. I didn't follow. I figured I was right the first time—one more argumentative female in a barroom. At that moment a cab pulled up and Crane stepped out. He looked after the girl.

"Our friend seems to be in a hurry," he said as he helped me into the cab.

"She's no friend of mine. She doesn't even like me."

"She hasn't given herself an opportunity to get acquainted," he said, closing the door and glibly giving the driver my address, remembered from that glimpse of my credentials.

Riding crosstown through the park, he chatted easily and amiably. The trip was a big improvement over my earlier journey that evening. I was feeling quite set up when he said good night at my door.

5.

THE clock said almost twelve as I let myself in the apartment, switched on the lights. The living room was homey and snug in the soft glow of the lamps, while the rain streamed darkly against the windows. I originally shared the place with another girl, but after she married I stayed on alone. Solo living has its advantages when one keeps such unpredictable hours as mine.

I ran a bath, got into a robe, and brushed my hair. It had been a big day and yet I didn't feel tired, but rather gay, almost in a party mood. I cold-creamed my face, stacked some cushions on the floor, and stretched out, with propped-up feet, to think about the case. But my mind kept wandering back to John Bartley Crane.

I'd never known anyone quite like him and I couldn't decide where he fitted. He was a gentle person, yet he had a hard streak in him, too. He'd mentioned the Navy, probably where he got that bad ankle, but he wore no discharge button. The only mark on his casually meticulous clothes was that stain. If it were blood, he could have got it from searching the body. But what was he looking for?

I was sure now that if Bette Alexander were the child of Ethel and Eddie Wells, there were no papers anywhere to prove it. Wurber had seen to that. Crane un-

consciously confirmed it . . . old friends of the family
. . . knew Sylvia when Bette was born. But somewhere
there was a tie-up.

I worried it around in my mind for another half hour
as I lay in the tub. I do some of my best thinking in a
warm, fragrant bath, but that night I only got drowsy.
I gave it all up and went to bed.

It seemed merely a matter of minutes when the buzz-
ing began, and persisted, boring into my subconscious.
I woke slowly, hoping I had been dreaming it, but there
it was again—the doorbell. The day was already faintly
light and quite clear. My clock said five-fifteen. The bell
rang insistently. I pulled on my robe and stumbled into
the foyer, called on the house phone.

A gruff voice said, "Hank Deery, Gale." I pressed the
door release, then ran into the bath, splashed cold water
on my face, hastily braided my hair. What did Henry
Deery, police detective first grade, want with me at this
hour of the morning?

I was wide awake when I opened the door to the
angular, sandy-headed cop, who as a rookie had worked
with my dad. His lantern-jawed face was solemn as he
followed me into the living room. I tried to cover a chill
of apprehension with a brightly light greeting. "What
do you mean, Hank, getting a girl out of bed this time
of day—if it's day. How's about a cup of coffee?"

Hank blocked my path and my chatter. "And how's
about what you know of a little punk named Eddie
Wells?" The apprehension spread, cold and fast, inside
me. "He was found with a hole in his head in a room on
Third Avenue last night."

My cold hands deep in the pockets of my robe, I

54

moved away from his indignant gaze. "What's the charge, Hank?"

"No charge, Gale, not yet, anyway. But Homicide says they have it straight from a dependable source you were in the murder house. You were there, in his room, not thirty minutes before the landlady found him— dead."

"And you told them you . . . you didn't believe it?"

Deery swore softly. "More than that. I told them I'd stake my reputation that you knew nothing about it, that if you so much as guessed such a thing, you'd call the precinct."

I could feel his eyes on me as I prowled around the room, switched on a lamp to warm the chill opalescent light of dawn.

"It was swell of you to go out on a limb for me, Hank, but it's true. I was there, saw the body, and I didn't report it."

His profanity took on a prayer-like quality. The admission made, I dared to face him, though it was harder to endure his disappointment than his anger. "This is true, too, Hank. I didn't kill him and I don't know who did."

"I wasn't thinking you killed him," he thundered, "but what kind of way is that to operate? Do you know you could lose your license? And I wish you would! A sweet girl like you in this dirty business, it's enough to make Jim Gallagher spin in his grave. You ought to have a home of your own and be raising babies." He stopped in front of me, his fists on his hips, his topcoat pushed back. "And now what am I going to tell the Inspector?"

I had been thinking of that myself. "You know my work, Hank," I said cagily. "I was up in that same neighborhood once before this week after a skip. Eddie Wells was one of the best. Agencies are looking for him from coast to coast. I got there too late."

I smiled but Hank scowled at me, in determined exasperation. "Is that all?"

"I came, I looked, I went. That's everything."

"Who was with you?" he barked.

"Apparently a tail from the department," I snapped. "O.K., so I wasn't alone. Dr. Wurber was with me. He has offices on the west side."

"So a doctor and a private investigator, two servants of the people, and you walk out and don't say a word to the police."

"Dr. Wurber will support my statement, Hank, that we found him dead. The doctor said several hours, at least. Neither of us wanted to get mixed up in it. We just left."

Hank said, "Where's your phone?"

"In the bedroom." If he really was going to give me a break, I wanted to make the most of it, and yet save his friendship. "How about that coffee now?"

Hank hesitated in the door I'd indicated. He tried to keep that Department look in his eye but he wavered, sighed. "I shouldn't take it, but I will."

I went to the kitchen and got out the Silex. I didn't like the look of this. It could be a ton of trouble. Wurber wasn't going to like it either. From the bedroom I heard Detective Deery giving somebody instructions concerning Wurber, then repeating my telephone number. A moment later he joined me in the kitchen, apparently more sad than angry.

"I told the Inspector I knew your father, Gale," he kept repeating, while I fried eggs and made toast. "I said you weren't one of these know-it-alls. You respected the Department."

I said nothing but I was thinking plenty. Just how much could I tell him? What could I tell him? What did I really know? I had a right to protect my client, Dawn Ferris. Would anything I did, or didn't do, actually endanger Bette Alexander?

The food on the table, I steered the talk to old friends, and the details of Hank Deery's lonely life since his wife had passed away. His mood was almost mellow when the telephone rang. I could hear only grunted ejaculations, as I poured him a second cup of coffee. His returning footsteps were heavy, and there was a puckered scowl on his face.

"Would you really be double-crossing me, Gale?"

I put the Silex down gently. "You know I wouldn't, Hank. I told you the truth."

"That's not what he says," he shouted suddenly. "They got Wurber on the telephone at his Jersey place. He says he hasn't been in New York for two days. The janitor at his New York house says the same thing. Now, what do you say?"

"It's my story and I'm stuck with it, Hank. He was with me." Unless, the wild thought dashed through my mind, that man was not Wurber. He assumed me to be Cora . . . I assumed him to be Wurber.

"Please believe me, Hank," I said when I'd coaxed

57

him back to the table. "I know nothing about this killing. I went there on another job entirely. It's an important, high-paying job for me, and different from anything I've ever done. I want to see it through. Give me a break, Hank. Don't drag me in on this Wells killing. You can cover for me—I know you can."

"And get broken, after twenty years' fine service?"

"Stall, Hank, give me time—that's all. I won't need much—perhaps even today will be enough, forty-eight hours at the most."

I did some earnest pleading in the next half hour while I threw in special services like another refill on the coffee and a light for his cigar. I wasn't making any progress. I'd broken one of the first rules of his life—report to the Department—and his trust was shaken. If only I could remind him that there were times when one must break rules, take chances—and suddenly I remembered.

"Hank, do you recall when you were working partners with Dad, your first year on the Force? He came down with the flu. The precinct was short-handed. You worked alone for a couple of days—and there was a whole rash of loft looting."

The scowl faded from his face as I started to talk, then he lowered his cigar and the tight lines of his mouth slacked a bit.

"You had some notion that something funny was being pulled off, but the Captain wouldn't listen. He was all for tossing you out to the farthest reaches of the Bronx for neglect of duty, but Dad came to bat for you. He helped you work on it, and you tripped up as clever a bunch of loft artists as ever lifted a bolt of silk. Remember?"

Hank put down the cigar. "I remember like it was last week," he said slowly. "But will you tell me how you know about it, you who was no bigger than knee-high to a mosquito at the time?"

"It was one of Dad's favorite lessons to me—one of my first lessons in crime. When a man's got a lead, don't push him. The time mightn't be now."

Puffing, Hank slid back his chair, rose. "I'm off until midnight tomorrow. I'm going down to Jersey to my daughter's. I'll give you your break, Gale. I'll make half a report on this, but . . ." He swung around and hit the table with his fist. "I'll make a full report when I come back."

"That will be eight o'clock Thursday morning," I said. "O.K., Hank, it's a deal."

"And then it's all you know—every word of it!"

"Every word, Hank—on my honor as a Gallagher."

Still grumbling, he struggled into his topcoat, then patted my cheek. "You should be cooking those fine breakfasts for some good man and not getting yourself into such a spot."

"You're a good man, but I'll consider the next decent offer," I promised him with a smile, but the smile drooped when I closed the door.

Hank Deery was right. I was in a spot. Someone had handed the Department a few facts that put me and my elusive companion on that spot. From where I stood it seemed the only man who could do it was John Bartley Crane.

6.

FOR a long time after Hank Deery left, I sat on the window seat watching the bright spring morning spread over the Manhattan sky, and did some dark thinking. That, Gale, my girl, I reflected, is the stuff that did you in—that spring trick, fuzzing up your reflexes and lousing up your work.

Spring and John Bartley Crane's charm had pulled a double cross, but good. I thought back carefully over every minute in Dario's, trying to recall each word from the moment we sat at that table until he left me at the door. He insisted that he wouldn't go to the police because it might endanger Bette. But if he hadn't, who had? Who else could have identified me?.

Yet, if it were Crane, he said nothing to the police to connect Eddie—dead or alive—with the Alexander case. Of course, Hank Deery could have been foxing me on that one. After all, I didn't tell him everything I knew either. I had never mentioned John Bartley Crane.

I prowled the living room, going one mental round after another without a decision. Then I stopped myself cold. This emotional shadow-boxing was a poor excuse for concentration. I wasn't thinking—I was just being mad.

I took a shower, dressed, made more coffee. By that

time my three morning papers had been delivered. I went through them quickly. There was no mention of the death of Eddie Wells. I didn't know if it was too late or too unimportant. Every day little people die violently in a big city without so much as a stick of print to mark their passing. But there was a half-column story about Bette Alexander on the first page of two papers, a two-column story with pictures on the third page of the tabloid.

In each paper the story was the same. They varied only in journalistic styles. It could have been covered in two words—nothing new. The pictures in the tabloid showed the gateway of the Alexander place where Bette was last seen. There was a shot of M. E. Baxter, the Alexander lawyer, leaving Queens General Hospital, where he had looked at the body of a girl recovered from Flushing Bay.

There was also a small picture of Bette's mother, Mrs. Theodore Alexander—this was Sylvia, a striking blonde, mature but potent. I looked at the picture for a long time. A posed photograph, taken before the kidnaping, it didn't tell much, except that here was a well-kept, well-fed woman, who at that time had nothing more to worry about than keeping her weight down. She was the type who would marry a man thirty years her senior. Her eyes were humorless, her mouth selfish; she looked as though she got what she went after, or maybe I was prejudiced.

In any case, I was thinking more clearly. Hank Deery had given me forty-eight hours to get out of the case . . . forty-seven hours, to be exact. It was now eight-thirty on Tuesday. And what was my job? To prove that Bette

61

Alexander was not the child of Eddie and Ethel Wells. If I could satisfy Dawn Ferris that Bette was Sylvia Alexander's own daughter, I was through. And the simplest way to get an answer is to ask a question—and as any newspaperman knows, the place to ask the question is right at the top. In this case, it might not be what they said but how they said it.

With a plan to follow I felt better. I got my car at the garage and went to the office. Patsy wasn't in yet. I looked over the mail, then turned to *Who's Who* for a thumbnail sketch of Crane, John Bartley. Born February 6, 1911—a little older than I thought. Lawrenceville and Princeton—he looked it. Studied art at the Academy in Philadelphia, Paris, and Rome. A list of awards. Lieutenant commander, USNR. It confirmed my impression of him, a mixture of sophisticated charm and unexpected toughness. I slammed the book. I had work to do.

Patsy breezed in as I was typing a message for her. "Gee, am I late? Such a push on that subway, I had to let two trains go by . . . I'm not late!"

"I'm early," I said. "I have places to go. Watch for all reports on Eddie Wells and get them organized for me."

"Do you think Miss Ferris will be in again? That was so wonderful."

"That's yet to be proven," I said. "I'll call you later. I'm driving out to Long Island."

"Swell day for it," she said wistfully. "It sure was pretty in Brooklyn this morning."

She'd have said it was downright gorgeous in Suffolk County forty minutes later when I left the Boulevard and took the road along the Sound. The water glimpsed beyond the wide lawns was a California blue. The grass was green, the young leaves were flourishing. Over low hedges I glimpsed beds and borders of spring flowers. The air was fragrant and soft as a bubble bath. It was a day that took resisting, but my resistance was set at a new high. Once my assignment was finished and my client protected, I would tell Hank Deery everything I could. And if ever I got into such a jam again, even for a slice of the United States Mint, I hoped someone would shoot me . . . which might happen before I got through with this one.

It was midmorning when I neared Huntington. As usual in these super suburbs the street signs were hidden by trees and there were no house numbers, but a police car served as marker for the Alexander place. A detective stopped me at the drive entrance. I showed my credentials, and while he consulted with his pals I got a good view of the place. It was impressive and depressive.

From the general sweep of it, I judged the grounds ran to acreage extending to the Sound. The wide lawn on either side of the curved drive was beautifully kept. The house, a large turreted affair, with bay windows and porches, had the shut-in look of country places built at the turn of the century. Giant box hedges blocked off the lawn in direct line with the north and south porches, shutting off all view of the rear. There was no sign of life, except for the representatives of the law who at that point rejoined me.

The officer handed me my wallet. "These seem O.K., but we have to know a little more. Who do you want to see and why?"

"I want to see Mrs. Alexander," I said. "The why is confidential." I gave him my best "we-understand-each-other" smile. He didn't buy it fast. I went on, being reasonable and pally, saying my client had some connection with the Alexander family.

Then offhand I said, "Is Terry Riley still out here at Oyster Bay?"

"You know Terry?" He called another arm of the law. "Miss Gallagher is a friend of Terry's."

A couple of minutes later I was turning the big circular drive in front of the house. Though I insisted I had no interest in the kidnaping angle, I kept thinking of Bette, the leggish colty child that Crane had described so fondly. Certainly it sounded fondly, I added to myself with irritation, as I parked my old heap behind a sleek new gray convertible.

I walked up the steps and pressed the bell and the door opened instantly. The flat-footed houseman looked like a cop to me. This must be the Wilson that Crane mentioned. I asked for Mrs. Alexander.

"Have you an appointment, madam?" he asked.

"No, but it is important—about the little girl." I handed him my card.

His fishy eyes quickened. "You have word of her?"

"No, I wish I had. This is another matter." His face relapsed into blankness. "Perhaps Mr. Baxter will see you. Please step this way."

I stepped across the entrance of the vast gloomy hall that suggested a museum before the days of indirect lighting, and entered a small stuffy period piece of a room. There was mohair upholstery and much bric-a-brac. Over the onyx and marble fireplace hung an enor-

64

mous painting of a heavy-jawed woman with high pompadour and neck-stretching collar. Her bright eyes glared down at me. I sighed heavily as if I'd eaten too many pancakes.

"You wished to see me?"

I turned quickly, faced a well-groomed man of possibly fifty. He wore a small mustache and carried horn-rimmed reading glasses and my card. He had the manner of a medium-priced mortician.

"Mr. Baxter?" He bowed slightly. "I really wished to see Mrs. Alexander, but you may be able to answer my question."

"You're on a case? You're here officially?" He waggled the card. "Who sent you?"

"I can't reveal the identity of my client, but we believe the answer to our question may have a serious bearing on the disappearance of Bette Alexander."

Baxter lifted his eyebrows in polite if apparently skeptical attention.

"Is Bette Alexander an adopted child?" I asked bluntly.

Baxter's eyebrows flew to new heights; his face was scarlet. "Adopted! Why, the audacity . . . Young lady, how dare you come into this house of grief with such a cruel question? If you are using your credentials to gain admittance with the hope of a sensational news story, I warn you it is libelous."

"I am here as a private investigator, not a newspaper reporter. I came to ask a question that could be most important to this case. Is she?"

"For twenty-five years I have been associated with *the family*," Baxter said, underlining the last two words.

"When my law firm assigned me to work with *the family*, Mrs. Theodore Alexander, Senior, was still living." He made a reverent nod toward the tough old girl over the mantel. "I have known Mrs. Theodore Alexander, Junior, since her marriage, and she would be most shocked at your question. I was—with them when Bette was born. I almost said present." He gave a sleety little smile. "Does that answer your question?"

"I take it the answer is no," I said calmly.

"Most assuredly." Having scolded me properly, he melted a little. "Now I am curious—why did your client ask such a question?"

"Her child was placed for adoption fourteen years ago. She thought she saw a family resemblance in the published picture of Bette."

"Is your client in New York?" Baxter asked, as he edged me to the door.

"Alabama." I named the first state that came to mind. I always find it easier to tell an offhand lie than insist honestly that a client's name, address, and history are confidential. Mr. Baxter opened the big front door for me, bowed me out.

I went down the front steps slowly. This trip had got me nowhere. It wasn't that I expected any great revealing answer. What I had been counting on was to watch Sylvia Alexander's reaction to my question. Baxter's indignant hamming meant nothing. He didn't impress me as the kind of person who had honest feelings, but rather the synthetic emotion required at the moment. I'd met men of this type before—the family custodians, who, like model children, react as their betters expect them to.

Actually I had my answer, I thought. John Bartley Crane's family had known the Alexanders for thirty-five years, at least. Montgomery Baxter had worked for them in this magnificent morgue for twenty-five years, was practically present when Bette was born. That should be conclusive, and yet—recalling pictures of Sylvia Alexander and the late Theodore, not to mention the late Theodore's late mother—I couldn't imagine their producing the gay creature who was Bette.

For a moment I stood by my car deep in thought. I was reaching for something that eluded me. In all conscience I could tell Dawn Ferris she was wrong. Every testimony denied that Bette could be her child, and yet, for my money, it still didn't add up. Like one of those tricks in mathematics where everything comes out nines —something is planted to make it work that way.

I was turning the handle of the car door when I heard the woman's voice—a full-throated voice with a touch of authority. I glanced around. There was no one visible between me and the officers down at the gate, a good city block away. "It won't be necessary, thank you," the woman said distinctly, and a door closed, a door with glass panes.

My ear followed the sound. It came from beyond the wall of hedge that shut off the rear of the grounds, only a few feet from the loop in the drive where I stood. Without a second thought, I ducked across the narrow space of lawn and wiggled through the mass of hedge.

The branches pulled off my hat, loosened my hair, and snagged my nylons—but I made it, emerging into a miniature forest. There were pines and blue spruce all about me, as I straightened up, adjusted the combs in

67

my hair, put on my hat. My hand on my hat brim, I stopped with a gasp of delighted surprise.

Through the trees there was a view as exquisitely unexpected as the inside of those marvelous Easter eggs Dad used to get for me. All frosted white and cold on the outside, a tiny fairyland within. This was a big fairyland. I was in a corner of evergreens that together with the hedge formed a background for an incredibly lovely garden, stretching out to meet the blue waters of Long Island Sound. That morning the garden was a riot of jonquils, daffodils, and varicolored hyacinths. Along the tanbark paths were a birdbath, sundial, and stone benches, while down near the water's edge was an old-fashioned summerhouse.

For a moment I was so entranced that I completely forgot about the woman until I heard her voice again— very close to me, but I caught only a fragment of sentence: ". . . dare to breathe." I had to get my bearings quickly. I stood very still among the trees, which were at the extreme southwest corner of the square outline of the garden, the house and the hedge forming the south and west boundaries. Another hedge and the Sound completed the square.

Except for the wall rising directly behind me, I couldn't see the house, but beyond the line of the ever-greens I glimpsed the gray flagstones of a terrace, from where the voice came. I inched forward, stopped at the sound of steps on the stones—a woman's quick light tread, a man's step, heavy and uneven. I froze right where I stood as they came into my line of vision and moved down the terrace to the path. A tall blonde woman in brown slacks and a tan corduroy jacket almost cut off my view of the very tall man in the blue coat and battered slouch hat, but he was unmistakably John Bartley Crane.

They turned away from me, walking east, then north along the path toward the Sound. They moved slowly, while she talked earnestly and his head was inclined as though he was deeply interested. Her voice was low now; I could barely hear a murmur even in the still garden, where there was no sound but the banging of my own heart. At snail speed they moved along the north path, quite obviously headed right around the square, which would bring them within inches of me. I couldn't retreat, couldn't move, without their seeing me. Therefore the thing to do was to be seen. I decided to wait until they were almost beside me; then I'd crash through as if I came in at that moment.

It seemed an eternity before they finally turned the west border. Sylvia was holding his arm and still talking. I could hear her voice now, a low steady murmur, to which he nodded. I was all set when, midway up the path, they stopped. He glanced at his wrist watch and said something to which she seemed in reluctant agreement. I almost could see her sigh. Despite her careful make-up, her face had a strained look, her shoulders under the boxy coat seemed hunched.

Had I not been watching her so carefully, I might have missed the next move. Her hand, drawn from her patch pocket, dropped into his; then he tucked something in his inside breast pocket. It looked like a wad of money. I couldn't be sure. Her voice rose and I caught words—"nothing" and "no amount." His hand gripped her arm in a gesture of encouragement.

69

Smiling, he took off his hat, that dark forelock dropping across his forehead as he bent and kissed her. She clung to him for a moment, then he went through a gate in the hedge that I hadn't noticed.

My emotions were doing a nose dive, but I righted them. This situation was made for me. Crane was gone and Sylvia Alexander was walking alone, toward me. I moved, ready to step in the path, ready to find out a lot of things. Suddenly something hit my head hard. I rocked. The next moment the only thing I knew was that the stars seemed to come out in midmorning . . . or was it midnight?

7.

VOICES and a big ache were spinning in my head when I opened my eyes. The light hurt so I closed my eyes again, but a man said: "She's coming to." Then closer to me: "Miss Gallagher . . . oh, Miss Gallagher."

I squinted up at Mr. Baxter, the Alexander lawyer, who was leaning over me, waving spirits of ammonia, which I hate, under my nose. I brushed the stuff away, sat up slowly. I was in a lovely morning room, all chintz and bright flowers and with another view of the garden. Gently I touched a tender place on the crown of my head.

"What hit me?" I asked.

"I did," snapped a gravelly male voice. "I hit you with a hoe."

I lifted my head a bit further. Beyond Mr. Baxter stood a lean old man with a great shock of white hair and a white walrus mustache. His bright eyes glared at me out of the bush.

"It's true," I mused gently, each word jarring. "One does see stars . . . firework stars. But who are you? Why . . ."

Mr. Baxter said, "This is Mrs. Alexander's father, Mr. Taylor. He thought you were going to attack his daughter."

"With my bare hands?" I asked ruefully.

"He didn't know you weren't armed," Baxter continued anxiously. "You better keep the ice bag on your head a bit longer. Then I'll get you a drink—or would you prefer tea?"

"I'm sure I'll be all right," I said. It always embarrasses me to cause a fuss, but that was quite a conk. My head still throbbed and my eyes played tricks, distorting my focus so that everything looked slightly bleary.

"You ought to call the cops, that's what you ought to do," Taylor was raging. "Nobody pays any attention to me. If you listened to me . . ."

He stopped in mid-sentence when the door was flung open. I was leaning back on the couch, the ice bag on my head, definitely not at my best, when Sylvia Alexander swept into the room. To the old man she said: "Hush, Pop!" To Baxter, "How is she?"

I said, "I'm doing all right."

Surprised, she spun around. At last I was face to face with the woman I had come to see, whose reaction I wanted to study, but I was in no shape to look, much less make profound observations. Fortunately her immediate reaction was too obvious to miss—she was plain old-fashioned mad.

"We should call the police," she stormed. "What do you mean, sneaking around private property like that? You should be thankful you weren't shot."

"I am—very." I took the ice bag off my head, sat up again, making another effort at recovering my poise . . . and my wits. "Perhaps you should call the FBI, Mrs. Alexander."

"That's what I say," Old Man Taylor roared, apparently forgetting which side he was on.

Baxter, hovering over me, murmured, "We don't want to do anything hasty, Miss Gallagher, but you were taking chances, knowing this house was under guard."

I said nothing. I was trying to think. Confusion seemed a natural state for the old man, but did I imagine that Baxter was trying to placate me? Was there an undertone of a signal to Sylvia? He was standing behind the sofa on which I sat so that I couldn't see him, but Sylvia, facing him, curbed her tantrum a bit abruptly, walked to the window, not, I was sure, merely to study the beautiful garden where she and Crane had walked. Baxter moved around to the end of the sofa.

"Where did you think you were going, Miss Gallagher?" he asked.

"Exactly where I got—to see Mrs. Alexander," I said, nodding toward her back.

"But why? I answered your question honestly."

Taylor snatched at that. "Honest . . . nobody's honest around here. Nobody tells the truth. Lies . . . lies, that's all they are. Nobody does anything about my little Bette, stolen, maybe killed."

"Oh, Pop, shut up!" Sylvia snapped, turning away from the window. The grand manner of the grieving lady that she had worn when she walked with Crane was gone now. She wasn't pretending. Even through my fog, I could feel her fear. It was in the tense set of her shoulders, in her darted glance toward Baxter, in her tone to her father. At the moment she didn't seem to be speaking to me.

Baxter was doing all the talking, in that same I-don't-want-to-be-too-harsh-with-you vein. But why? I kept wondering, as I slowly gathered myself together, finally got to my feet, trying my balance and my ideas out at the same time. Actually the old fellow was right. They should call the police and the FBI.

Wilson, the tough-looking houseman, called Baxter to the phone at that moment. At the door, Baxter glanced at Sylvia with a look as final as the period to a sentence. She returned to the window. I dug my cosmetic kit from my coat pocket, tottered to the big mirror over the fireplace, and slowly began a reassembly job. I was pretty thoroughly wrecked.

I couldn't have put my impressions so clearly at that moment, but I was gathering a picture of Sylvia Alexander that was to remain with me. She was handsome in a big, bold-featured way, with prominent eyes like her father's and big, beautiful, predatory hands that didn't have a born-to-the-manner look. She wasn't born a blonde either, but had a smoothly expensive job that included eyebrows and lashes. Sylvia Alexander was a lot of things today that she wasn't in her youth, including rich and a lady . . . part of the time. She was having trouble with the role right then. She was also having trouble to keep quiet.

Standing before the mirror, trying to comb my hair with hands that couldn't get together with my reflection, I said: "I realize I handled this very badly, Mrs. Alexander. You and Mr. Baxter have been most kind."

She turned in that quick way of hers. "I didn't even know you'd been here, until you fell at my feet, scaring the soul out of me. Where did you come from?"

74

"Through the hedge from the front drive," I said, steadying one hand with the other as I drew on a fresh mouth. I felt better. Strange how much confidence a little make-up can give a girl.

Sylvia moved across the floor. There was an odd mixture of caution and eagerness in her profile, reflected in the mirror before me. She was looking at me, quite unaware that I was also looking at her. There was momentary hesitation in her manner, indecision in her eyes, as I put on my hat. Then, as if she couldn't control it, she blurted out: "Why didn't you use the side gate?"

Still apparently studying my own reflection, I asked casually, "Is there a side gate?"

There was a sudden eagerness in her face—and her voice. "Yes . . . yes, there is," she said brightly. "If you'd come in that gate . . ."

Mr. Taylor, filling his pipe from a humidor in the corner, grumbled: "Stranger around here . . . how you expect her to know . . . crazy place . . . what difference how she came in?"

It made a lot of difference to Sylvia Alexander. Since I didn't know there was a gate, she assumed I had not seen John Bartley Crane leave by the gate. And if I hadn't seen him leave, I hadn't seen him at all. As I suspected, that tender little pay-off was a private affair. Suddenly she was gay as if she'd been reprieved from the chair. She was actually cordial as I moved away from the mirror, faced her.

"Now about your original question, Miss Gallagher. Mr. Baxter told me about it when you were brought in. It's really ridiculous. You can tell your Alabama client that Bette is my own child."

There it was—the statement I wanted from Sylvia Alexander, flung at me like a challenge. There was no argument about it. I either had to take her word for it, or call her a liar . . . for which I had no real reason. This case needed a Queen Solomon, and at the moment I wasn't up to it.

Taylor took a puff on his pipe, snorted. "Craziest thing I ever heard. Wasn't her grandmother right there when Bette was born? Me, I went to sea till 1939, but you can't deny your own flesh an' blood. Bet's the spittin' image of my own mother."

"I'm really very sorry this happened." Sylvia was buttery now. "Father must have thought you too were a kidnaper."

"Never thought such a thing," he retorted as I was putting on my coat, "and you know it. Always did say it was an inside job, but nobody listens to me."

I was listening to him as Sylvia was asking if her chauffeur could drive me back to town, or if there was anything she could get me.

"I would like to have that cup of tea Mr. Baxter offered me."

"Of course," she said. Her smile was attractive, not warm but good-humored, the kind that went with a gal who would be swell when she had it. I reflected, as Sylvia strode out of the room, that she was also one of the few women who look good in slacks.

The old man still stood belligerently in the middle of the floor. I crossed to the coffee table by the sofa, a matter of inches from him, lifted the lid of a cigarette box, then glanced at him and smiled.

"May I?" I asked.

"Oh, sure, sure." He took up the table lighter, held the flame for me. I gave him a very personal smile. He said, "Not mad at me?"

"No, I think you were very resourceful, Mr. Taylor. I had no business coming in that way. But aside from my client's interest, I've been following this case on my own. Bette must be wonderful."

"Nobody like her. Her father was a stuffed shirt, and Sylvia . . . well, she's my daughter, I guess, but she's an awful fool. Can't see when she's being rooked, right to the eyebrows. But anything for geegaws and show."

"You are a very discerning man, Mr. Taylor. Perhaps Bette takes after you."

"I always figgered she did," he beamed. " 'Gramp, we're pals,' that's what she'd say. Oh, Miss Gallagher . . ."

His face behind all that bush seemed to crumple, and for a moment I thought he was going to cry. But there wasn't time for a big scene. "Look," I said, "about this inside job . . . you may have something. You're interested in the child's safety. If anything happens—anything at all—call me."

I put my card in his horny old hand, which shut like a mousetrap, crushing my fingers. There were tears in his eyes. "Miss Gallagher," he began—and finished. Baxter came in one door as Sylvia came through the other, followed by a maid with a tea cart.

I said, "I didn't quite get a light, Mr. Taylor." He chuckled as he snapped the lighter again. There were rainbows in his eyes and a sudden catch in my throat. That kid had something . . . a great deal of something.

That thought kept me company as I drove back to town—that and a number of others. Just what did give between John Bartley Crane and Sylvia Alexander, with whom he'd got chummy so very recently? And a lot chummier than he'd implied last evening, judging from that garden scene. And why the pay-off? Any amount, she'd said. For what? Silence, perhaps. She was blonde, and a blonde had been to see Eddie Wells while Crane stood across the street. He didn't mention seeing any blondes, but then—there may have been a lot of things he didn't mention. Maybe the old man had something about an inside job.

I didn't like that angle, but unpleasant angles have a habit of being the right ones in this business. If Bette was Sylvia's child, where was the tie-up? Certainly she seemed to be Sylvia's own baby. There were more people at that birth than might be expected at a wake. And where did Eddie come in? Was he putting the bite on Sylvia? Did Crane really know him? Had Eddie ever met Bette?

Then there was the way that Baxter eased me out of that house. There was that signaling that must have gone on over my groggy head. As executor of the estate, did he know about the money that Sylvia handed Crane? Why that sleight-of-hand exchange in the garden, unless she was holding out from someone in the house? Sylvia had called to someone in the morning room, as they came out on the terrace. Was that Baxter? Or her father? Perhaps the old man was doing some snooping on his own when he came up behind me.

By the time I drove across the Queensboro Bridge I had two headaches. I also looked pretty disreputable, all mussed up and no knees in my nylons. I drove directly to my apartment, stopping only to pick up the afternoon papers. At home, I poured myself a shot of straight Scotch, started a hot bath running, then called the office.

Patsy had a string of reports, some personal and routine stuff, a lot of reports on Eddie Wells, and no word from Dawn Ferris. "But I'll be nice to her if she calls," Patsy assured me.

"Is that everything?" I asked.

"Just about. Oh, yes, I got the photostat on Bette Alexander's birth certificate."

"Read it to me—all of it," I said.

While she got the report, I flipped through the papers. On the inner page of the *World-Telegram* I found a tiny item. A man, tentatively identified as Edward Wells, was found dead of gunshot wounds in a rooming house at 9028 Third Avenue. The police were investigating.

Patsy chirped in my ear. "I got it, Gale." She read the familiar data off to me: Elizabeth Anne, female, May 5, 1933, 8018 Fifth Avenue. Father: Theodore L.; mother: Sylvia Taylor.

"Everything I already know. Is that all?"

Patsy hesitated. "There's a doctor's signature. Lemme see . . . Wiber—Weber—no, Wurber, A-l-o-i-s Wurber."

So he was there, too! The doctor who attended Sylvia Alexander.

"Anything else you want?" Patsy asked.

"No," I said quietly. "That is really everything."

8.

SO Dr. Alois Wurber signed the birth certificate for Bette Alexander! Lying in a foamy hot bath, I rubbed my bruises and reflected on the amazing peregrinations of Dr. Wurber. That gentleman surely got around.

He attended Dawn Ferris, the erstwhile Mrs. Wells, delivering her daughter on May 5, 1933, of which there was no account except Dawn Ferris's word. On the same day, according to the record, he delivered a daughter to Sylvia Taylor Alexander. He had known Eddie Wells and quite obviously was acquainted with Sylvia Alexander. Did he also know John Bartley Crane?

Crane had said: "You knew there was trouble or you wouldn't have brought a doctor." Was that a guess on the basis of the bag that Wurber carried—or did Crane know him? Had Crane turned me in to the police, and if so, why hadn't he mentioned the connection with the Alexander case? Certainly Sylvia Alexander and the lawyer Baxter weren't anxious to have me hobnobbing with the gendarmes.

Wrapped in a robe, I fixed myself some lunch, continued to worry the thing around over a pot of tea. Relaxed and fed, I began to pull a plan into shape, but it was like taking over a bridge hand half played, with no idea who holds the tricks. A little finesse was in order.

As a starter, I found John Bartley Crane's number in the book and dialed it. Perhaps his memory would be as short as Wurber's and he would have forgotten our previous meeting. Perhaps he already had a report on my visit to Huntington that morning.

"Bart Crane speaking." The pleasant crisp voice came practically in mid-ring. I had my brightest tone ready.

"Oh, hello, Mr. Crane. This is Gale Gallagher."

"And this is a pleasure," he said, sounding as if he meant it. "I was going to call you later. Heard any more of our departed friend?"

I told him about the item in the *World-Telegram*.

"Apparently the police have not connected his death with—anything else." He was being cagey. "I . . . I wanted to talk to you today, Miss Gallagher, but I'm expecting an important phone call and can't leave the studio. Do you suppose you could drop by here?"

"I'm at my apartment," I admitted. "I came up to change for a dinner date. I could drop by briefly, though —say in about an hour?"

"Fine. I'll be waiting."

I replaced the phone thoughtfully. The guy definitely had a way with him. He was the kind who could make any female, any age, believe she was the only person who mattered to him. Apparently fourteen-year-old Bette was caught in that spell—though he made it sound as though he were the spellbound one. Obviously he had Sylvia Alexander doing ground loops, but me now . . . I jumped up and pulled off my robe. I was going to keep my head on my shoulders and my feet on the ground.

In the bedroom I selected my favorite item for a

semiformal dinner date. It was a brown silk faille suit dress with a taffy-colored satin blouse. Brown may not be a spring shade, as sales people are always telling me, but it's my color any season of the year. It does things for me. When I added triple-sheer nylons and high-heel pumps, a slightly mad hat and my beaver jacket, I liked the effect so well I was sorry I really didn't have a date for dinner.

Before I left the apartment I called Patsy again for a late report, but there was nothing new. I gave her Crane's phone number in case of emergency. Then I sailed out, with a feeling of cautious adventure, for Crane's apartment—three blocks away.

Bart Crane opened the door for me. In old slacks and a soft flannel shirt, he was every inch the society artist at home. He was also the gracious host—also bigger and even more attractive than I remembered. His apartment was attractive too, spacious, masculine, and comfortably disordered. As he took my jacket, in the softly lighted foyer, I glimpsed a living room to the right, but he opened a door to the left.

"Half of this is a conventional apartment," he said, "but I do most of my living in the studio."

I preceded him into a long cluttered room, the north wall of which was one huge window. I crossed to the window, using the view as an excuse to get my bearings and the feel of the place. The view presented a fascinating assortment of roofs and towers. In that first glimpse, I saw a woman on a penthouse terrace, wash hanging from a fire escape, a man lounging in the window of a loft building, a church spire.

"One could scarcely call it pretty," Bart commented.

"No matter what you call it, it's Manhattan and I like it."

"So do I," he said with that special tone of touching sincerity.

He placed a chair for me near the window—a comfortable chair, not too deep or too high. From a forest of chairs against the wall he had picked my size exactly. It might have been his artist's eye or more of that charm. He offered me Scotch from a handsomely practical little bar, made from a Victorian washstand, black walnut with a marble top.

"My grandmother had an entire bedroom suite like that," I said in happy recognition. "It was her first American purchase, when she was a bride of eighteen right out of Wexford, Ireland."

"Have you ever been to Wexford?" he asked, handing me the drink. "Very beautiful country."

"It's one of those things I've promised myself for the future. So far, I haven't had time."

"You seem to be a very busy lady."

If that was a lead, his expression gave no indication of it. He poured his own drink, sat facing me in a long deep chair that fitted him. The huge confused room was coming into focus now, and I realized that there was plan here—oasis of order in what at first seemed total chaos. I looked pointedly at the covered easel.

"You, too, seem very busy."

"I am. I'm doing Prunella Van Damm right now. She had a two-hour sitting this afternoon." He stretched out a long arm, flipped back the cover on the easel, revealing a sketch of a cherubic little girl. I exclaimed in honest pleasure. It was really lovely—not only pretty, but warm with the glow of childhood.

"That's why I like to paint children," he said. "You can put down what you see because all children are lovely. It's the pattern they chose to follow—or that is thrust upon them—that spoils them. Pru, there, will be a little monster at seventeen—probably a neurotic alcoholic at thirty."

"What a dreadful prophecy," I said, looking at the charming child with the shy dark eyes and soft mouth.

"I hope I'm wrong, but with a million-dollar inheritance, she's neglected, unloved, and insecure."

"Is Bette Alexander like that?" I asked.

"Oh, no!" He leaned forward eagerly, those capable brown hands linked around his glass. "Bette has great inner resources. Some people seem born without them, as they might be born tone-deaf or color-blind. Then, too, people, like horses or dogs, can be overbred. The strain gets too thin, as in Pru."

"Bette is not an aristocrat?"

"To me, she is of the only true aristocracy . . . the exclusive society of great souls. Actually by birth," he interrupted himself to light a cigarette, while I waited, my breath caught, "by birth," he resumed, "she comes of rugged stock. Her grandmother, Sophie Dobbs Alexander, was quite a character."

That was the tough old girl in the gilt frame in the Alexanders' reception room. "I told you my family had known them very well. Sophie's father made a fortune in textiles. A strong-minded gal. She was a drug on the marriage market." He grinned. "She wouldn't take those who'd have her and couldn't get those she wanted.

Finally a scholarly bachelor named Theodore Alexander came along. She married him after they had both turned forty, and they had the one son. Her husband died within ten years, but she had no more need of him than the female spider."

"That one who eats her mate?"

"Sophie achieved it theoretically. She did a pretty good job on her son, too. In her spare time she doubled the family fortune with her real-estate investments and continued her husband's studies on the life and times of Alexander the Great."

"And you think all this contributed to Bette's personality?"

"Certainly." He was quietly confident. "Then there is her mother's family . . . sturdy middle class."

From my impressions of Sylvia Alexander that morning, I'd have said lower middle class. Actually I said nothing. Bart refilled my glass and went on to prove his point and make it all add up to the girl that was Bette Alexander.

Was it a deliberate picture—because he knew I had been to Huntington that morning, asking the question I had tossed to him so casually the previous evening? This gracious hospitality, that reference to a proposed phone call—was it another way of calling off the dogs?

The telephone rang and Bart leaped to answer it. I still liked the way he said, "Bart Crane speaking," but from the fourth word I could tell this was not the phone call he expected—merely some routine social thing that he disposed of quickly.

While he talked, I kept prodding myself. I needed prodding. It was so comfortable, so easy to forget why

85

I came. With Bart Crane it was easy to talk, even better to listen. He had a deep interest in people, an interest that in most persons stops somewhere between idle curiosity and vicious gossip. My interest in people I acquired from my father. Dad had no opportunity to study history, much less psychology, but he wanted to know what made people go—right or wrong. Bart Crane knew the answers without ever seeming smug or pompous. Dad would have liked him.

I dawdled over my drink, and gazed out at the soft mauve spring twilight crawling like a curtain over the city. The magic of the thousand tiny lights sprang up in offices and apartments while a spear of light spread across the sky from some near-by beacon.

Suddenly Bart, coming noiselessly behind me, said, "This is what I meant."

He sat on the floor beside me and spread out a dozen sketches—a folio of Bette Alexander. There in black and white she came alive before my eyes, this lovely girl with the winged eyebrows, the upturned nose, the wide passionate mouth, changing from infant to woman in a turn of the head, a lift of sweeping lashes.

I could hear again the quaver in Noah Taylor's voice describing her. "Gramp, we're pals." Bart saw her like that too, honest, direct. But still I couldn't see the heavy, frustrated Theodore Alexander and the selfish, greedy Sylvia Taylor producing this child.

As I turned the last picture, several small sketches fluttered out on the floor. Bart gathered them up. "May I see those too?" I asked.

He was looking at them almost tenderly. "They

aren't mine," he said. "They are things Bette did. She could copy anything."

Bart dropped them in my lap and I turned them carefully. They were a child's clever mimicry in line. She captured the detail if not the spirit.

"She drew some of them sitting in that chair," he said. "Bette used the broad arm for a desk. She always sketched while waiting to be called for."

"She was called for?"

"Of course, either her mother or Monty Baxter. Once I drove her home."

"Bette never went around town alone? Many girls of fourteen do."

"Had the family lived in town, she certainly could have, but someone always brought her in from Huntington." He gathered up the pictures. "If you're thinking that she could have known anyone outside the family circle—someone like Eddie Wells—you're wrong. Besides, the police and the FBI have been over this detail. They know every move she made in the past three months."

"Then how does Eddie Wells fit? What was he after?"

"From his record, I'd say he was apparently trying to make a soft touch; a common enough background for kidnaping, as you must know."

"Then you think his death was merely coincidental?"

"If there were any connection, the police would have found it," Bart said brusquely.

"They are good—but not mind readers," I murmured half to myself as he carried the folio off to some shadowy corner of the studio.

I rose. It was nearing six. I had to get along, but I lingered at the window. The scene was really beautiful now, the harsh outlines softened and blended in darkness, with the arc of pale sky above.

I leaned against the heavy folds of the monk's-cloth curtains. For a moment I was tired and discouraged. I had come here to find out several things: whether Bart had reported my call on Eddie to the police, whether he knew of my visit to Huntington that morning, and why Sylvia Alexander had given him the money there in the garden.

Yet not for one moment had Bart tipped his hand, and I couldn't ask directly without tipping mine. His attitude on Eddie had changed since last night. Eddie knew Wurber . . . Wurber knew Sylvia. Was there a link? And just how much did this man know?

"You look very lovely standing there," Bart said in my ear, his hand against my arm, with a touch that was vibrant and strong through my sleeve.

I whirled to face him, and words, sudden and uncontrolled, blurted out. "Why did you kiss Sylvia Alexander this morning?"

The silence was a terrible thing . . . and cold as the hush in the arctic wastes. I stared at him in sheer numbed shock at my own words. Where had they come from? How could I ever have said such a thing?

For a moment we were both paralyzed by the awfulness of it; then Bart moved, stepping back, away from me. The lines of his face were set slick and hard, like a mask—a polite mask. He switched on a lamp and then another and another—as though we needed light. All

I wanted was something deep and dark to swallow me.

"You really are a sleuth, aren't you?" he said icily. "Every pose a trap."

That hurt. If there's one thing I don't go for, it's posing. Standing by that window, I never thought how I looked, or what I had on, or even that he might be thinking about me.

"I am a sleuth," I said, with a ragged remnant of pride, "but I try to be as honest as the business permits. Don't judge all women alike, even if many do pose for you—in and out of your profession."

"This was a professional call?"

"And why else do you think I came?" Good hot Irish wrath was covering my embarrassment when the telephone rang. Bart grabbed it up instantly as I started for the door.

"It's for you—your office," he said.

I turned back quickly. My office after six? Patsy never left a moment later than five-one. But it was Patsy. "Gale, I'm just leaving. Miss Ferris is here."

She gave a small rhapsodic sigh. "She's getting me tickets for the broadcast and Joan Crawford's autograph."

"That's ducky; but where is she now?"

"In the reception room, waiting for you. She says it's very important."

"I'll be down in ten minutes," I said.

"You don't mind if I go now, do you? I got a date for eight o'clock."

"Run along. I'm sure Miss . . ." I caught up the name in a gulp, "won't mind waiting alone."

Bart was at the door holding my jacket. As I slipped into it I said, "I owe you an apology, Mr. Crane. I had no intention of asking such personal questions."

"It's quite all right," he said coolly. "I didn't answer the question."

9.

THE ceiling light from my reception room glowed through the transom as I came down the corridor from the elevator, blasting my hopes that Dawn Ferris had not waited for me. I certainly didn't feel up to facing her right then, but I put on my most confident look and opened the door swiftly.

Dawn Ferris was sitting on the bench, exactly where I had first seen her, little more than twenty-four hours earlier. It didn't seem possible that I'd been on the case only twenty-four hours, or that so lovely a woman could have brought so much trouble. And lovely she was—in a teal-blue gabardine suit with a whole herd of foxes over her shoulders. But the fear was still in her eyes and there was something more now—a drowned look that might have been despair.

However, our mutual emotions and reactions were wrapped bright as Christmas gifts as we exchanged greetings. With apologies for my delay, I switched on lights, led the way to the inner office.

As I hung up my jacket Dawn crossed the room to the desk with her poised actress's walk. I had a hunch it was definitely an entrance to a scene she had in mental rehearsal while waiting for me. Her first line was an ad lib.

"You look perfectly stunning, Gale."

My thanks fell short of being gracious. I was reminded too sharply of Bart Crane's compliment. It didn't matter how I looked. I turned it off quickly, getting right to business, as I settled at my desk.

"I have a lot to tell you," I said, "and yet it all adds up to nothing—so far."

Dawn perched on the edge of the chair, facing me. Her jeweled hands clasped her bag, gloves, and a yellow paper that looked like the file copy of our contract. She kept that bright, bright smile turned on full blast.

"I'm sure you've done your very best, Gale, and I do appreciate it. That's why I waited for you. I could have left a message with that sweet little Miss Higgins, but I wanted to talk to you."

"What did you want to talk about?" I didn't like the quality of her smile combined with that look in her eyes.

"Frankly, I behaved very foolishly." She was giving me the penitent-girl routine. I leaned back in my chair, braced for a blow. Something was coming—but good.

"Just how do you mean?"

"I allowed myself to become hysterical over nothing, Gale. I'm sure now it was entirely my imagination."

"You didn't dream up that letter you showed me," I said, "and Eddie Wells shot through the head was real, too. He is really dead."

"Eddie dead? How awful!" Her smile flickered and went out. Her reaction told me nothing.

"The whole thing is terrible," I snapped. "Stop acting, Dawn, and tell me the truth. What's happened?"

Without the smile, she looked tired but more natural. "Nothing's happened, Gale . . . nothing. I knew Eddie was dead. I read it this afternoon."

"Is that why you came here?"

"No. This has nothing to do with Eddie."

"It all has a lot to do with Eddie—somewhere. He was murdered and a blonde woman was seen leaving that building."

Dawn sprang to her feet. "I wasn't there. I don't even know where he lived. And I tell you this has nothing to do with Eddie—it's only that I came to my senses, and realized that Bette Alexander could not be my daughter."

I drew a deep breath. She was doing an about-face. Somebody had called the orders. Very quietly I asked: "Why are you so sure?"

"Oh, a dozen reasons. I can't really explain." I missed that quick level look of hers I'd noticed on our first meeting. She wasn't looking at me now. "I simply know, that's all."

I rose, came around the desk, and stood before her. "Yesterday you gave me a large fee to determine what became of the child you bore in Dr. Wurber's hospital fourteen years ago."

"That wasn't what I wanted at all," Dawn denied petulantly. "I only wanted to be sure that my child was not Bette Alexander—and now I'm sure."

"And now you're lying."

Dawn caught her breath, as if struggling with a denial, and continued in a tightly reasonable tone, "I paid you that fee for an investigation. I am now satisfied in what I wanted to know. The money is yours. The case is closed. Do I make myself clear?"

"The words are clear but they don't make sense." I walked back to my chair. "You can't be sure, Dawn, because now I'm not. Yesterday I rather thought you were whipped to hysteria by a collection of odd coincidences. Today I think there is a large chance that Bette Alexander is your daughter."

"No—it can't be! I won't have it!" Dawn jumped up, leaned toward me.

"Now you're hysterical. Sit down and listen to the facts that I have."

Dawn resumed her place on the edge of the chair; her shoulders under the foxes were rigid. She would listen, but I could see my words would make no difference. I still had to say them.

"There is no record of the birth of your child, Dawn, but on that same day Dr. Alois Wurber signed a birth certificate for a daughter born to Sylvia Alexander, in the apartment they occupied at that time on upper Fifth Avenue. I met Sylvia Alexander this morning. She is a distraught woman and I don't think her state is due entirely to her anxiety over Bette."

"You went there—you really went there?"

"Of course. I went there and asked if Bette were adopted. They denied it. Sylvia's father, Noah Taylor, and their lawyer, Montgomery Baxter, according to their story, practically witnessed the delivery. But everybody has too many irons in the fire. They're playing games. They seem to be doing everything except trying to find this child."

Dawn stood up. She was very pale. "I'm not playing games, Gale. I'm in dead earnest and it's because of

Bette. She's in danger, terrible danger, and for that reason you are to drop this case."

"You know where she is? You know who has her?"

"I know nothing except what I just told you. You must close the case."

"But I can't. I'm in it up to my neck. I have one more day before the police will take over. And when they do, I'm going to tell them everything. You're my client. You paid me well. If I could break this, and save you the publicity, I would, but I can't get out of the case."

Her blue eyes were cold and hard. Her chin—so like Bette's—was set as she stood close to the edge of the desk, looking down at me. "You really mean that?" she asked quietly.

"I have no choice. The thing's a time bomb. You can't stop it. It's bound to blow."

Slowly Dawn drew her big purse from under her arm and the shelter of the foxes. My eyes followed the soft hands, while I felt a sharp catch in my middle, remembering that other purse and the glimpsed gun. My hand reached toward the side drawer, but she was quicker—coming up with a cigarette case.

I swallowed my heart, declined her offer of a cigarette, went on more urgently as she lighted her own.

"I don't know who got to you, but believe me, Dawn, this is no way to protect that child."

Dawn merely looked at me through the smoke of her cigarette.

"You thought no one knew your identity except Eddie. Now Eddie is dead—but someone has reached you . . . and it wasn't through me." There was a mo-

95

mentary flicker in her eyes as though that thought struck home. I persisted: "Don't be a fool, Dawn. The police are working on Eddie's murder, and they're thorough. They'll track back and eventually catch up with you. Stay with me on this."

Except that she was smoking, she might have been an elegant figurine in the window of Saks Fifth Avenue. Whatever the conflict in her mind, it was completely hidden behind the mask of that lovely face. Even her eyes betrayed only fright. It was plain no dice.

"I'm sorry you won't go along with me," I said, "but actually, there isn't anything you can do about it. Since I've been on this case I've been spied upon, lied about, hit over the head, threatened by cops, and perhaps," I frowned, recalling that wretched scene with Bart Crane, "offered a bribe in an odd sort of way. I'm right in to my eyebrows and I'm either going to drown or come up with the answer."

Silence. I pushed my chair back, stood up. "At least we understand each other, Dawn, and you'll know why I do what I must do. If it comes to a showdown with the police, I am protected. I have your agreement as my client."

"I suppose some people interview you but do not engage you."

The apparently irrelevant remark took me by surprise. I didn't expect small talk now. "A few," I said. "People shop for investigators as they do for any service."

"Then that's what I was doing—shopping," Dawn Ferris said, her eyes suddenly fever bright. "I never engaged you. I never paid you a cent. Have you checks to show the transaction?"

"No, but I have a contract that you signed."

"Do you?" The lighter was still in her hand. Unlike any lighters I ever owned, it flared instantly under her touch. She swept the flame across the yellow paper she'd been holding and tossed the sudden blaze into the big metal ash tray on my desk. For a second it writhed in a horribly human way, then collapsed in black ashes.

"What was that?" I asked.

"My contract," she said triumphantly.

"How did you get it?"

"I told your little Miss Higgins I wanted to read it again and she obligingly gave it to me. That was the reason I waited for you. If you wouldn't give up the case —and I was afraid you wouldn't—I wanted you to see me destroy that paper. Then you couldn't blame the poor kid too much."

Dawn dusted her fingers daintily, pulled the foxes around her. "Good-by now." Her voice sang and her smile was practically radiant as she sailed out of the door.

I sat there listening to the click of her heels going down the corridor, the rumble of the elevator door; then the stillness of after hours crept through the building. I looked earnestly at the Benton landscape and heaved a big sigh.

There were no two ways about it—I was out on a large lonely limb. Wurber said he wasn't even in town the previous evening when we found Eddie's body. Now I had no evidence that I'd ever been engaged on the case in the first place. Patsy had seen the contract, but

97

Patsy worked for me . . . or did she? I reflected wryly.

I wasn't angry with her. Why should I be? The poor kid was touched with the special adolescent insanity— star worship. It was all my fault. I had played the whole thing stupidly. I saw that paper in Dawn's hand when I came in—and she'd been too smart to tuck it out of sight guiltily. She let it sit right there in front of me for twenty minutes.

I'd been stupid with Bart, too. I couldn't forget the surprised look in his eyes. Was it because of what I said? Or that I knew about Sylvia? It couldn't have been because he meant it when he said I looked lovely. I ran my hand over my soft faille skirt. It was a stunning suit. I'd dressed deliberately, lied about the dinner engagement as an excuse to wear it, and then forgot that it might be effective. Being a girl is a full-time job; any other profession louses it up . . . and vice versa.

I jumped up angrily from the desk, reached for my jacket as the telephone rang. I stopped, the jacket in my hand, waiting. It rang again, shrilly loud in the quiet office. I snatched it up.

"Gale? This is Bill Conway. I'm in town between trains. How's about letting me entertain you for a couple of hours?"

Bill Conway's breezy voice brought back quick memories of pleasant wartime dates, dances at the officers' club at Quonset, parties at New London.

"Oh, Bill, you angel, what timing! Do I ever need to be entertained!"

We settled on a place to meet, and ten minutes later I had repaired my face, locked the office, and was on my way. I locked my mind, too. I wasn't going to think of the Dawn Ferris–Alexander case for two hours. But as I stepped in a cab, I did have one flash of backhanded, totally illogical satisfaction. It was the thought of Bart Crane and the fact that I did have a date for dinner!

Three hours later, as I headed for home, I literally felt like a new woman. Nothing sets a girl up like a couple of champagne cocktails, good food, and the attention of an attractive man—even if he did talk mostly of his fiancée in Seattle. Bill and I had been strictly playmates, with no carry-over in the heart department.

Now I was happy because he was happy with another girl. As I walked down the softly lighted hall to my door, I wondered about that—not for the first time. Was it really normal for a girl to be so palsy, so bighearted? Shouldn't life at twenty-six consist of more than sending my men friends on their way while I chased missing persons and uncollected bills?

Thinking about it, I turned the lock and opened the door. As the door closed behind me, I was stopped still, my hand on the knob. I caught a strange scent combined with the awareness of another presence. The wide windows made a square of rose-gray light from the night sky, outlining the curtains, the cushions on the window seat, the edge of the wing chair. My hand moved toward the switch.

"You may put on the light, Miss Gallagher, but don't move or make any sound."

The switch tumbled under my finger and light flooded the room. Sitting in the wing chair, facing me, a gun in his pudgy little fist, was Dr. Wurber.

99

10.

FOR a second I stood braced against the door, confronting the nasty little doctor. Then gradually my fear slipped away and I laughed.

"The little man who wasn't there," I said. "Stop pointing guns at me. I'm not going to scream and you're not going to shoot me."

He put the gun in his pocket, while his eyes traveled over me. "You're looking most attractive."

"I must have looked like a hag yesterday," I retorted, as I took off my jacket and hat. "How did you get in here?"

"What a question from an accomplished housebreaker like yourself!"

"I didn't break into your office. I was admitted."

"I didn't break in either." He jingled a bunch of keys. He was oozing confidence from every pore. Was it he who had scared Dawn off? Was he really in on the snatch? I took a cigarette from the end table, lighted it, curled up on the love seat near the door—all very deliberate, while I got my wind and my bearings.

"So you know who I am now," I said.

"The police are charmingly blunt. 'Gale Gallagher says you were with her this evening.'" He gave an unpleasant chuckle. "I told the absolute truth when I said I never heard of the lady, but their statement had prepared me for what was to follow. I further said I had not been to New York last evening. Dennis supported my statement because he did not know I was there. He did not hear me come in or leave."

Dennis would be the Irish janitor who had protected me from the foggy, foggy dew.

"With the situation so well in hand, why did you come to see me?"

"Because," he made a tent of his stubby white fingers, "as I demonstrated to you last night, I am a kindly man."

"Definitely."

"I want to be your friend, Miss Gallagher," he continued, adding the impossible to the improbable. "Today I checked up on you. I found that your father had a fine record with the New York Police Department and died in the line of duty."

"How does he figure in this?" I snapped. I didn't want Wurber even talking about him.

"It is part of the picture," he went on. "I found that you have operated your unusual little business capably and honestly for several years. Your work was not trailing the felon, but concerned chiefly with locating missing persons. There we have something in common."

"I've never *caused* anyone to be missing."

He shook his shiny head chidingly. "You do not understand. In my own way, I've righted many social wrongs."

"I make no such pretense."

"You underestimate your work. If you return property to its rightful owner, a missing husband to his wife,

101

a lost child to its parents, are you not contributing something to human happiness?"

"Very little. But I'm sure you didn't come here to sell me on the importance of my work."

"In a way, yes," he said. "It is a very unusual profession for a woman, and I admire what you have done." His high-pitched voice took on an edge of ice. "I should hate to see you lose it."

I didn't stir from my corner of the small sofa, but my heart was beating faster. The cards were coming down. "I don't believe my business is in any danger," I said.

"But you are in great danger." Was this the routine that was handed to Dawn? Wurber leaned forward, his hands on his knees. Somehow I never could get those hands out of my line of vision.

"Danger? From whom?"

"That I do not know," he murmured. "But this afternoon I had a call from a former client." He paused and I waited, totally dead-pan, though it wasn't easy. "Sylvia Alexander."

"I know you delivered the child called Bette. I have a photostat of the birth certificate."

His brows came together briefly, and more of the oiliness leaked out of his voice. "Mrs. Alexander told me of your visit to her home."

"Did she tell you I got hit on the head?"

His squeamish little smile was affirmative. "See what I mean? You walk into danger. They'd have been within their rights if they'd shot you."

But they didn't even turn me in, I reminded myself. I wasn't in danger from legal angles or violation of civil rights. The danger came from darker things than that. My cold fingers slid together, felt the need of clutching tension, but I realized the telltale gesture in time, dropped my hands, palms up in my lap. Wurber was watching my every movement and his gaze became a bit more penetrating, a bit more wary just as his tone became faintly sharper.

"Mrs. Alexander is ill with worry over her child, considering all the double dangers a girl of that age could face." He leaned forward in the chair again, his small shiny shoes pointed downward as if about to take off in a pirouette. "Isn't that sufficient agony for a mother without being questioned on her natural rights to that child?"

"If there is a question on those natural rights, this is certainly the time to bring it up. It could have a bearing on the case . . . the fortune left by Theodore Alexander, or . . ." I met that marble eyed gaze and held it deliberately, "or the death of Eddie Wells."

"There's absolutely no connection."

"You speak with authority."

His white face got whiter. "I knew Eddie Wells slightly. He was a weak, whining, conniving little chiseler. It requires brains and desperate courage for anyone to execute a kidnaping today."

I grinned. "That courage count puts you in the clear—and as for brains, I've had too much police training to think that any criminal is basically smart, any more than that any criminal act can pay off."

"You're being a fool—an absolute fool," he cried, his voice shrill. "You're in a big game, with fortunes and lives at stake. If you're smart, or even sensible, you'll get out. You'll tell your client to go back to Alabama or wherever she came from, and forget the whole thing."

Was this a fishing expedition? Didn't he know about Dawn Ferris? I clamped my teeth together to hold my tongue, but my icy routine was getting him.

"Every kidnaping case has stirred up false claims of all kinds—the Matson case, the Lindbergh kidnaping. You should know that."

"Sure, everybody wants to get in the act," I said. "You and Sylvia Alexander and Eddie Wells and perhaps my client from Alabama."

Wurber was on his feet. "She has no claim—absolutely no claim. I have the papers. I have every proof of Bette Alexander's birth. You saw the papers. Show them to her."

"Some people don't believe everything they read, or everything they're told. We're like that—my client and I." I rose then too, slowly, deliberately. In spike heels, I was eye level with the doctor. "I don't scare easily, either. I was engaged on a specific assignment and I'm staying until I get an answer that satisfies me."

Wurber's fat shoulders shook with rage. His slick smooth face took on a slightly blue shade. I was scared, but even with the little gun in his pocket, I had to believe he was more scared than I.

"You're mad," he was shrieking. "You're asking for destruction. But I don't want to be destroyed. I won't be." He stamped his little foot like a spoiled child. "I won't stand by and see all I've worked for, all I've accomplished, destroyed by you."

"You must have heard that the seeds of destruction are within oneself. Nothing would please me more, Dr. Wurber, than to upset your carefully constructed baby

104

market. I didn't set out to hurt you, and if you are innocent, I couldn't."

We were standing face to face, so close I could feel his moist hot breath on my cheek, but like an animal trainer, I didn't dare give an inch.

"I know you delivered that child," I repeated, "but it wasn't of Sylvia Alexander."

His hands shot upward, hovering like white bats. I caught my breath so sharply my diaphragm ached, my throat closed under the imagined touch of those hands. For seconds I waited for him to strike; then suddenly, with a great gasping sob he let his arms fall to his sides.

"How much do you want?" he whined brokenly. "I have money—plenty of money. I'll pay you well to drop the whole thing. You're young. You like pretty things. I'll give you more than you can make in a year."

I heard the whistle of my own breath as I stepped backward—not daring to turn my back on him. "I'm not for sale, Dr. Wurber."

"But this other woman—she must be young. She must need money."

My heels bumped against the chair. I sank into it, crossing my knees to stop their trembling. The game was over. I had won. If he didn't know she didn't need the money, he didn't know my client was Dawn Ferris.

"You must ask her," he was insisting. "You can't refuse for her."

"I have refused, Dr. Wurber. There is nothing further to say. If you'll pardon me now . . ."

"The police will deal with you, that's what will happen," he fumed. "Obstructing justice . . . interfering . . ."

We both started as a buzzer sounded. "What was that?" Wurber demanded.

"The downstairs door," I said, taking a crabwise course to the house phone in the foyer. "Probably Lieutenant Deery from Homicide."

"Oh, for heaven's sake!" Wurber squealed. "I don't want to see him." He snatched up his neatly folded overcoat and homburg from the window seat. "How do I get out?"

Holding the house phone, I leaned against the wall and pointed to the service entrance in the rear of the small passage between the foyer and kitchen. Wurber scurried out, and the patter of his feet running down the stairs echoed back to me from the door just before it closed. As I kept saying hellos into the house phone, I thought what an accomplished escape artist Wurber really was. But one time he would fail. Such acts always did.

Warily I moved to the front door as the bell rang. Taking no chances that time, I lifted my revolver from the drawer of the telephone table and set the small bolt chain on the door before I turned the lock. The door swung open a brief three inches. Looking down at me through the narrow space was Bart Crane.

"At least you show some discretion," he said, as I released the chain and managed to keep the gun out of sight.

"I've had quite an evening," I said. "I'm particular as to whom I admit."

"Thanks." There was no indication in his manner that he even recalled those last few moments in the

106

studio—or that there was anything to recall. He walked into the living room as though he were not only expected but invited. By contrast to the neat doctor, Bart dropped his hat and coat on the love seat, selected the deepest chair for himself. The wing chair that Wurber had occupied was my favorite, but I was sure I'd never sit in it again—certainly not until the furniture cover was laundered.

Bart said, "It's a bit late for a call, but I wanted to talk to you. I phoned you at eight."

"I was eating chicken Divan at the Divan Parisien," I said as I crossed the living room to the kitchenette beyond.

The strain of the past hour was catching up with me . . . a strain to which this sudden visit was a topper. My head was spinning, and my heart was no help. I needed a drink. I poured myself a double Scotch, swallowed half of it before I asked Bart what he'd have.

"Anything—with a little soda or plain water." I poured Scotch for him, too, brought the drinks into the living room. He was looking at three small watercolor sketches grouped near the window.

"You have excellent taste, Gale." The name meant more than the compliment. The glasses on the silver server in my hand rattled.

"I know what I like even though I couldn't say why," I managed calmly.

"Intuition," he said. He took the drink, murmured his thanks. He seemed just a bit too casual as he resumed his place in the deep chair. I retreated to the love seat, beside his hat and coat.

"This has been a very strenuous day," I said. "I'm tired. So if you can be brief, I'd appreciate it. Of course, you probably want me to lay off the Alexander case."

"Psychic as well as intuitive," he said. "You admit now that you are on the case. Last evening you were merely dunning the late Mr. Wells."

"I tipped my hand to you this afternoon. It can be as embarrassing to have too many aces as not enough."

"That can even prove fatal," he said quietly. I straightened up and looked at him.

"So that was why you came—to call me off the case. Apparently I don't know my own strength."

"What do you mean?"

"Three times today I've been ordered to drop it." I finished my drink, put the glass down so hard it cracked. "Well, I'm not quitting."

"I wasn't ordering you, Gale. I was merely suggesting—for your own good."

"Oh, yes, it's always for my good," I snapped, my Irish steaming. "Everyone is taking such good care of me all at once." I sprang up, moved restlessly around the room. "There's danger . . . big, dark danger. I don't know what I'm up against. The hell I don't!"

"I wouldn't be so sure. There's a very definite danger—even though I don't know the source."

I stopped before him, my arms crossed, cold hands hugging my elbows. "What are we fighting—the Phantom?"

"Someone a bit more solid and concretely menacing. The stakes are high in this game. Kidnaping carries the death penalty, and to point out the obvious, a man can hang only once."

Or a woman, I added in my mind, as I moved away from him. "You weren't talking this way this afternoon," I said. "Why have you switched your approach?"

"The approach, as you call it, has nothing to do with the case." That grinning tone was in his voice for a moment. "Other things developed after you left."

"You got the phone call."

"I had a visitor—Sylvia Alexander."

I wasn't surprised. "She had a busy day, too."

"A very disturbing one. Bette has been gone five days. Each has been a personal hell of anxiety for her mother, realizing the girl's double danger. It didn't help to have you asking questions regarding Bette's parentage." He finished his drink leisurely, deposited the glass quietly, even smiled in questioning permission as he took his pipe from his pocket. So correct—so damned correct.

"I realized too late," he continued, packing the pipe, "that all your questions last night and this afternoon— at least, most of them—concerned Bette and her forebears. I merely thought you had the child's interest at heart."

"If I do, I'm the only one," I retorted angrily. "Everybody has fish to fry. Bette—her life, her safety— is the last consideration, even of Sylvia Alexander. She was panicked this morning, until I implied that I had not seen you two together in the garden. Well, I had— I saw it all."

"What do you mean—all?"

"Exactly what I said. I came in considerably ahead of your fond farewell with Sylvia in the garden. I saw her give you the money."

"You didn't mention that in our last skirmish."

"And why should I? When it comes right down to it, what do I know about you? A society artist who paints modish moppets for fat fees. All this tall talk about Bette could be so much lip service."

I couldn't forget Noah Taylor's chattering that it was an inside job. I was convinced that Bette was not Sylvia's child—but had Sylvia told anyone? Pacing the room and glancing at Bart's cool, distinguished profile, I didn't know. There was so much I didn't know, but of one thing I was sure: I was close to the truth, judging from the pressure brought on me that day.

I couldn't forget, either, the presence of this man. He filled the room, charged it with a new and disturbing element. I was too tired to fight against it. I could only wish he hadn't come. Yet when he glanced at his watch and rose to leave, I knew an irritating wave of regret . . . for what?

"You have reason to doubt me, Gale," Bart said, still disgustingly calm as he got his coat. "I don't have too many reasons to trust you. Perhaps after tonight it may be different."

"Nothing's been changed. I told you I wouldn't give up my angle on the case."

"You need rest. These have been strenuous hours for all of us—and surprising." He belted his navy coat and picked up the battered hat. At the door, his hand on the knob, he looked back at me. "Personally, it's been most disturbing. I think," he said slowly, "I'm in love."

The door opened and closed. He was gone. Angry and confused, I glared at the paneled wood. Was this part of the act, or was it straight? I put on the dead latch and the chain, my fingers fumbling unsurely. I so terribly wanted an answer. I almost wanted to cry.

Switching off lights, I went back to the window seat, pressed my face against the cool pane. Maybe Wurber was right. The game was too big for me. Perhaps my efforts were putting Bette in what he called double danger. Double danger . . . the words buzzed in my tired mind, striking another echo that I couldn't trace.

Numb with weariness, I stared down at the quiet street. A cab wheeled to the curb before the house. I saw broad shoulders and a battered hat disappear into it. Bart must have been tired, too, if he couldn't walk a few blocks on a fine spring night. If he were going home . . .

I sat upright, suddenly wide-awake. The talk of the evening ran through my mind like a played-back recording. Double danger . . . Bart said that, and so had Wurber. Bart had been waiting for a phone call and he got it. Someone had used that phrase to the two men— or one had used it in speaking to the other. It was too much of a coincidence that they both would have hit on this particular combination of words.

"After tonight it may be different," Bart had said. Because tonight would be the end. He wasn't going to his apartment, he was going to contact the kidnaper.

All at once the entire situation clarified, like the drop of the proper chemical in a cloudy liquid. The kidnaper had undoubtedly made a second contact with what Montgomery Baxter called *the family*. That explained the money Sylvia gave to Bart, her anxiety at my presence, and the reason she hadn't turned me over to the police. She had not reported this second demand for ransom, and was afraid of what I might have seen, what I might say, that would tip the police.

Wurber also was in this, somewhere. I couldn't believe he was the kidnaper, but he had something to do with it. That was why he wanted to buy me off—before something I knew, or he thought I knew, upset the whole deal. He was afraid, desperately afraid. Why? Then the logical answer came to me. He had Bette! She must be there in his house.

I dashed into the bedroom, stripping off the faille suit. As I changed, I could hear his shrill voice, see him bouncing with hysteria, a man mad with fear. If the slightest thing went wrong, in the contact or the pay-off, or if the law appeared in force, Bette wouldn't have a prayer. But perhaps he wasn't that afraid of me—perhaps!

11.

IN spite of my preoccupation, I was amused at the look the taxi driver gave me when I named a hotel on Broadway—the shabby place in front of which Wur- ber and I had got the cab on Monday night. Apparently few people really used it for living purposes, even during the housing shortage. But the name stuck with me and served as a good destination close to Wurber's house.

I had changed to my working clothes—the belted all-weather coat and the Knox hat. I have found it the perfect outfit for my purposes. It's so inconspicuous that no man gives you a second look and any woman assumes you're going to work—forgets she saw you. I could be any of the women who work through the night in a big city—waitress, telephone operator, nurse, small-time entertainer, or—from that look of the taxi driver —even a call girl.

As I sat in the corner of the cab, my hands deep in the slash pockets, my fingers made nervous doodles on the objects they touched—the wallet and flashlight in the left pocket, the gun in the right. My weariness of an hour before was gone. I was wide-awake—almost too wide-awake. I wished I were not quite so aware of cer- tain angles of this excursion.

I had no business in this thing and I knew it. If Hank Deery found out about this, he personally would see that I lost my license . . . and he'd be right. I was doing all the things I swore I'd never do, including holding out on the police department and working on a case that included a major crime angle.

But I couldn't have stopped if I'd wanted to. Not only did I believe that Bette's safety depended on me, but there was my professional reputation—and possibly my life. I was in a web woven by some very desperate people, and who held those threads I didn't know.

The cab turned off 57th Street into Broadway, only a nod from Bart's apartment. I was convinced now that Bart was go-between in an undercover attempt to pay the ransom, but I kept shying away from considering several other angles that lurked in the back of my mind. Dark possibilities that all this between Bart and Sylvia might not be free of deeper intrigue. People have used such methods before to bleed estates.

Then there was Sylvia's interest in Bart. He was younger than she, but not more than a few years. She was handsome, and though she didn't inherit the principal of the Alexander fortune, she would get a fine income for life. When Bart said he had fallen in love, he might have been talking about Sylvia—or just talking. I was glad to see the dingy hotel ahead.

I paid off the cabby, moved slowly across the sidewalk as he drove away. At one o'clock the neighborhood was quiet. As a sailor and a girl went into the hotel, I went around the corner and down the street toward Wurber's house.

Suddenly I was in the midst of commotion. A girl,

114

very drunk, was seated on a doorstep on the opposite side of the street, and insisting to her escort and the entire neighborhood that she was going to spend the night right there. I didn't like that. Noisy drunks draw cops.

I cut my walk down to a crawl, seeming to watch the unhappy spectacle across the street. It gave me an opportunity to observe the few cars parked in the block. The big car with the New Jersey license that I noticed the night before, and assumed to belong to Wurber, was not in sight. One more step and I was on the sidewalk in front of number 47—the doctor's house. The place was totally dark from basement to top floor and looked as formidable—and impregnable—as a fortress. I went a little cold just looking at it.

At that moment a man with a bulldog on a leash came down the steps of the rooming house east of number 47. He walked toward me close to the curb, his interest apparently absorbed by the drunk's performance, which was getting broader and louder by the second. Several others had stopped to watch her, and even a taxi slowed down in passing. No one was paying any heed to me.

Right then I was wishing that Manhattan had back alleys, which provide such a convenient and private means of exit—and entrance. But this house did have a narrow passage separating its east wall from that of its neighbor, and intended for a service entrance. For the benefit of anyone who happened to glance my way, I stepped briskly into the passage, as though it were my rightful destination.

The place was darker than a pocket, and smelled of

dampness. I dared one quick look with my pencil flashlight to get my bearings. Like most of such passages, it sloped downward slightly, coming out on a level with the cellar kitchen at the rear. Two large ash cans and a garbage pail were lined along the wall. At the rear was a wooden gate, about chin-high to me.

As I reached the gate I heard a car stop in the street and a voice of authority mingle with the squawking protests of the drunk, then a shrill laugh, footsteps—quiet. The car started up again. Authority won.

And if you had any sense, Gale, my pet, I told myself, standing quiet and uncertain in the smelly corridor, you'd have authority not only on your side but by your side right now. But I'd started this on my own, and I was going to end it that way. If I got in this house and found Bette Alexander, I'd be made—or finished.

The gate, I was sure, led into a back yard, but peering over it, I could see nothing. I could climb it without too much trouble, but I first tried the old-fashioned drop latch and the gate swung open with only the faintest squeak.

I closed it noiselessly, waited while my eyes became accustomed to the variations of darkness. The yard, illumined by the glowing overcast from the city, was much lighter than the passage. I could distinguish outlines, a small square of cement surface surrounding a small circle of earth in which grew a sister to the Brooklyn tree. Meeting the rear of the property line was an enormous black wall, towering up some six or eight stories and extending a quarter block in each direction, apparently the back of a warehouse facing on the next street.

Against the wall, an oblong of light was silhouetted suddenly from an upper room of the house next door. The light was a help as I moved forward cautiously, following the line of the fence. Dennis was a fine caretaker. The yard was pin neat, not a twig or a scrap of paper on the ground. The only thing in the yard beside the tree was a large square stone flowerpot, once very fashionable adornment for the front steps of such houses as this. Now it stood, gloomy as an oversized funeral urn, against the wall of the house.

I stopped at the angle of the fence, out of the line of light from next door, and studied the rear of the house. It was as dark as the front, but not quite so formidable. There were French windows opening on a small balcony at about half-story height above the ground. This was the main floor of the house, probably had been the dining room at one time, but now—as I knew—was Wurber's private office, that neat room with the files. Were those windows wired for a burglar alarm? I doubted it. Wurber called on the law no more than necessary.

But just how sound a sleeper was Dennis in his downstairs apartment? Was I standing right outside his bedroom at that moment? Was he alone? Was he watching me? I was taking fool chances. I knew it; but I had no intention of turning back. I moved around cautiously to where the big square flowerpot stood against the house. It was heavy and solid, and approximately three feet high—just tall enough to give me a lift to reach the grillework on the side of the balcony.

I hadn't exactly been training for hounds and hares that day, but I made it, landing safely enough on the balcony with only a popped garter and an unduly rapid pulse for the effort. At that moment the light went off in the building next door, blotting out landmarks I had only just established. The next instant another light went on, hard and bright, highlighting me like a spot.

I flattened myself against the French doors and looked up. The light came from an unshaded side window in that busy house next door. A young fellow clad only in shorts crossed the room, with that peculiar preoccupation of persons unaware that they're observed. He went out of view, came back again, carrying a bottle of beer. The light went out. I stood in the darkness, waiting, lest he were standing in the darkened window looking down at me.

Then I felt the pressure of the metal door catch in my back. I wondered what type of bolts this door had. If it were only a slide blot in the center, it could be easily managed. I turned the latch, pressed to gauge the point of greatest resistance. The door slowly swung open.

My fingers tightened on the latch and a chill went up my arm. This was too easy for comfort. Had someone been watching me and opened the door? The caretaker, Dennis, or that other go-between? My legs were stiff and awkward, but I edged through the door with tiny sliding dance steps, holding myself rigid as though I didn't like my partner.

The memory of Dr. Wurber's office was clear in my mind: desk in the center, file cabinets with the gooseneck lamp to my right now. I drew the door closed behind me, not taking a chance on its banging in the first breeze. I pulled it firm, holding the latch tight until it snapped, then releasing it gradually. It locked with a bang like a .45.

I pressed against the door frame, my ears aching with listening, but I could hear no other sound, had no feeling of another presence in that blackness. I slid a trembling hand across the door. It was locked firmly now. Beneath the curtains I could feel a long rod, a special kind of lock for fastening double doors. I had seen them before but had no idea how they worked. Even simple mechanics puzzle me; anything as complicated as this floored me entirely. One thing was certain, I couldn't go out the way I came in—quickly.

But I wasn't concerned with leaving right then. I had other things to do. With my arm held up as a shield, I continued in that slow sliding movement. I figured I should touch the files in about ten steps from the window. I kept my elbow ahead of me in an easy up-and-down fan motion, but there wasn't even a sense of anything but space.

Then suddenly something touched my leg, coiled around my ankle with a faint crackling sound, and clung. I stopped in mid-step, my toes pressing the floor with sudden simian skill. Somehow I managed to swallow a scream while the thing against my ankle moved like dry fingers. It took an act of will to bring my arm back, force my cold hand into my pocket, and find the little flash. I pointed it downward, shielding it with my coat. Then it took me another moment to realize what was coiled around my foot. It was a large piece of thick brown paper—the kind used for padding carpets. A dusty bundle of the stuff was loosely rolled there on the floor.

I swore in sheer relief as I bent to extricate my foot. Then my eyes traveled out of the tiny circle of light around me. Something was wrong—something in that brief glimpse was different from my mental picture of that room. I steered the light across the floor and saw a dim pattern of dusty parquet. This floor had been covered with a linoleum rug . . . waxed linoleum. I could almost feel it again under my feet as the memory came back to me.

Straightening up quickly, I forgot caution, waved the light around. The room was empty, totally empty. There was nothing in it but the curtains on the French doors. I crossed quickly to the light switch by the opposite door. It clicked under my fingers but nothing happened. There was no light.

I stopped, trying to quiet my mounting panic. Had I got in the wrong house? Entered the wrong passage by mistake? That wasn't possible. The passage I took was between Wurber's house and the rooming house next door, where right now a young man on the third floor was finishing a bottle of beer. No, this wasn't my mistake. The conclusion was plain. Wurber had moved that day.

Wurber was a fox. Perhaps last night, while I talked to him in this room, Bette was upstairs. After leaving me at Eddie Wells's, he could have come back here, tucked her in rugs in the big car, and whisked her off to New Jersey, under the very eyes of the cops. Or he might have taken her out of here this very night!

Me and my smart ideas! Wurber probably came to see me that evening before I got the bright notion of coming to see him again. He needed time—a very little time—and I was the only one who threatened it. And I couldn't even be sure what that threat was.

Half sick with disappointment, I stood for a few moments against the wall. I suddenly was tired and shaken, as though every nerve had a frayed end. Of course, there was nothing to do but get out of there. I straightened, then stopped at a sound—a squeak of a board . . . another . . .

I was standing beside the door to the big reception room. I turned the knob, let the door swing open. My eyes, now accustomed to the darkness, found the softer shadows that marked the big curtained windows at the far end of the room, and a thread that could only be described as less black, showing that the double doors to the hall were open, and giving a glimpse of the vestibule glass. I inched around the door frame, listening. Had I leaped to conclusions too rapidly? Was it only this floor that had been emptied out? Were the rooms upstairs occupied?

My gun in hand, I waited. I'm a good shot, but a gun never gives me confidence. I've never had to use one on a case, and I was not sure now that I could. I took another step. There was a loud squeak. Was it the board under my feet or another person's foot? I waited, frozen in one position, for what seemed an eternity.

A car rolled by in the street, then silence again, thick muffling silence. If only I could see, but except for those two faintly gray spots, the room was a black cavern. This room was empty, I could feel the hollowness of it; but was there someone in the hall, or on those stairs?

I didn't dare flash my light, make a target of myself, and yet the waiting became unendurable. Dad always said women were too impatient to make good detectives. So I had no patience! So I had to take my chances!

At least there was no question of explaining my presence now. If anyone else were in this house he had no more right to be here than I did—or at least as much reason for concealing his presence.

With a deep breath, I started diagonally across the room, my eyes on that sliver of light in the vestibule. I moved quickly and quietly over the smooth bare floor. The double doors were almost within reach, when suddenly my foot struck something and I pitched forward, went headlong, hitting my chin on the floor.

The gun shot out of my hand, scrapped noisily over the boards. For a second I was stunned, my hands, knees, and chin burning from the impact, my wind knocked out by the bulk I'd hit. A roll of carpet, I thought groggily, as I started to pull myself up. Then I felt the sticky wetness of my left hand.

My damp fingers froze in position while my right hand reached awkwardly for the flashlight, turned it on. Gradually, as if hypnotized, I recoiled from the thing over which I had fallen. The round bulk was covered by a coat, a man's belted coat. I rose slowly, my hand still squeezing that light, pushing the small circle forward, bringing each detail into focus. The shoulder, the sleeve, an outstretched arm with a pudgy white hand, like something about to crawl—crawl into a darkened pool.

The arc of light from my flash gleamed now on the round face, the twisted lips, and the bulging dead eyes of Dr. Alois Wurber.

My own voice, echoing through the empty house, startled me into reason. It could have been one shriek, or it might have been going on for an hour. Time had no meaning for me. Then gradually the sound brought me back to my senses and to my danger.

For a while I crouched on the floor, my right fist tight against my lips, forcing myself under control. I still heard squeaks in the house, but I was now sure it was only boards, like old people, murmuring in their sleep. If the person who killed Wurber was still in the house, I'd have been done in long since.

At last when my voice and legs could be trusted not to scream or collapse, I got to my feet, used my scarf to wipe the blood from my hand. I was sure it would never feel clean again. Shuddering, I wadded the scarf and thrust it reluctantly into my pocket. I was more numb than composed, but it served as a satisfactory substitute for courage as I moved forward, weaving my flash over the humped figure on the floor.

Wurber had been shot in the chest and throat, but he hadn't died neatly and quickly like Eddie Wells. He'd fallen, rolled over, and, judging from the position of his left arm, tried to raise himself. Much as I despised him, I felt a great pity for him. He didn't want to die. His pudgy, unpleasant little hand, which always repelled me so, was stretched out as though clutching at something there at the edge of the pool of drying blood.

I bent down with the light. There was something in his hand. It was a small ball-point pen. The arm had shot forward in that last fall, and the pen left a long streak on the floor now partially covered by blood. Cautiously I moved around. Anything he was writing would be close to him, but I didn't want to move the body—for a number of reasons.

However, I made myself lift the edge of his coat with my light and peered under it to where his arm would have rested had he raised himself to write. There was no paper in sight, but moving the light as close as I could I found that streak again, heavier now. My interest served to blunt slightly my repugnance. I lifted the sleeve and the heavy arm, tracing the streak backward. There directly under the body on the floor was the start of the message. Excited, I leaned closer.

His handwriting was unmistakable—that square script that I had seen on all those cards. He had written only the beginning of a word, three letters that deepened the chill already possessing me. Gor . . . The little curve after the "r" ended in a broken stroke, then plunged ahead in that uncontrolled line that ended in blood. Gor! What was it? Who was it? His murderer? The kidnaper?

I felt that mounting tension of hysteria in my throat again. I set my lips hard and backed away. I had to get out of there . . . out through the door that the murderer had entered sometime after eleven o'clock that night. This time Wurber hadn't found an exit. He had come face to face, I was sure, with the murderer of Eddie Wells. The technique of the killer was the same—simple and direct. Whoever it was walked in and blasted, then left by the back way—accounting for those doors so magically opened for me. If I had been earlier, perhaps twenty minutes, half an hour . . .

Pushing that thought out of my mind, I walked with careful steps into the hall, found my gun where it had hit the far wall after flying out of my hand. I stooped to pick it up; my fingers touched the cold metal when through the silent house echoed the shrill, strident ring of the doorbell.

12. AT the sound of that bell, I dropped right where I was, at the far side of the hall, my light doused, my heart hammering. The ring was repeated, authoritatively, as though this person expected admittance.

From where I crouched, the vestibule door that stood opened inward at an angle hid my view of the front door with its frosted glass panels. A shadow against the glass might give me some idea of this midnight caller . . . a man . . . a woman.

The ringing was now supplemented with a knock of metal on glass; a heavy ring struck against the pane. Perhaps this person couldn't hear the bell, or this might be the signal of an expected visit. It couldn't be the police. They never knock fancy.

The very thought of the police set off a skyrocket flare of panicked thoughts in my mind, one trailing the other. I had admitted being with Wurber when I found Eddie Wells, but Wurber had denied he even knew me. I was telling the truth, so his denial might have been broken down, but now I was here and Wurber was dead. How would the truth look?

The knocking was accompanied now by a rattling of the doorknob. Somebody wanted in for sure, somebody who knew Wurber was here. I had to get out, but could I ever get that French door open again? I started across the hall on my hands and knees. My heart was pounding so violently my breath tasted bitter in my throat. Perspiration that chilled me ran down my back until my blouse clung frostily.

It wasn't a very wide hall, but it seemed a mile between that wall where my gun hit and the yawning entrance to the living room. Any moment I expected the front door to yield to the pounding. I got past the open vestibule door and took one quick look over my shoulder at the front door beyond. Out of the dark, a great white light leaped at me, big as the headlight of a locomotive.

For a second I was blinded. Head lowered, eyes shut, I stumbled to my feet, ready for headlong flight, while bright spots whirled against my lids from the glare. I struck against the edge of the vestibule door as I rose. I opened my eyes then. The light was gone but I couldn't believe what I saw.

There against the side panel of the front door was a face, peering through at me. A man's face, sharply clear in the reflection from the street light at the corner. I swayed against the edge of the door for a second, still not trusting myself, until he lifted his hand again, struck the glass with a large handsome ring.

It was Bart Crane!

With a cry I rushed to the door, pulled the bolts and locks and chains. Bart turned the knob and pushed the door open, then pulled up sharply at the sight of me. I was absolutely gibbering, but his glare of angry amazement braced me a little. I backed away, straightened my hat as he shut the door behind him.

"Why the devil did you come here?" he demanded.

"Never mind that now, but when I saw you through the glass . . ."

"Through what glass?"

"The door." I pointed behind him. "Didn't you see me?"

He glanced at the panels. "I didn't see anyone. I even used my big flashlight trying to look in. It's one of those one-way glasses. Wurber could see out, but no one could see in."

"Thank Heaven I could see out. Oh, Bart, I don't know what to do."

"Isn't Wurber here?"

My teeth were chattering. "He's here, all right," I said. I told him quickly. Gripping my arm, he steered me through the hall into the big room. His large electric torch caught that body in one swift bright wink.

"That is . . . was Wurber," I murmured, looking away from the huddled form.

"Your introductions come too late," Bart said wryly, walking slowly around the dead man.

I didn't think this was the moment to tell him that had he been a bit earlier, or Wurber a bit slower, he'd have met the doctor at my apartment that evening.

"Did you come here to meet him?" I asked, unconsciously talking in a whisper.

Bart turned abruptly. "Never mind that now. Let's get out of here."

I moved toward the door, stopped. "But I can't run away—not again. We've got to call the police."

"There's no phone in here now," he said harshly, grabbing my arm. "Let's get going."

He hurried me into the early morning quiet of the street and headed toward Broadway. The sudden change was almost more than I could take and I wobbled on my feet. Bart's relentless grip steadied me, kept me going.

"Might have got yourself killed," he was grumbling. "I kept looking and looking for some trace of life. I didn't know what had become of you."

We were nearing the corner. I stopped. "Became of me? You knew I was in there?"

"Certainly. I was standing across the street, right behind that brawling barfly, when you came along. After half an hour, I decided to go in."

"Half an hour," I murmured weakly. "You mean I was only in there half an hour?"

"That seems to have been long enough," he said grimly.

We were in front of the shabby hotel again. Bart hailed a cab. I crept into it, sank gratefully into a corner, as he gave my address. If this driver gave us curious glances, I was too weary to notice.

Bart slumped down beside me, that ancient hat on the back of his head, a scowl on his face. He lit a cigarette, handed it to me. The very effort of smoking steadied me a little, but I was really whipped. Defeat, disappointment, and shock tangled with sheer physical exhaustion, leaving me too spent to think or to speak.

Presently Bart grumbled, "I still don't know why you came."

"I thought *she* was there," I said flatly. "Now I don't know what to think. I was so sure . . ."

"He's the one you were with last night." Bart made

129

a statement out of it. I nodded. "You certainly get around," he said.

"It's my business," I reminded him defensively.

Another silence, then he asked, "What kind of voice did he have?"

"Rather high . . . could be oily, but went shrill in excitement or strain." I glanced at his thoughtful profile. "You talked to him?"

"Perhaps."

"Then you were . . ."

Bart glanced warningly toward the driver, shook his head. I relapsed into silence. What good were questions now? I was really out of it. I was thankful when the cab slowed up at my door.

Bart told the driver to wait, then he hurried me in, like a parent dragging home a runaway child. Too heartsick and tired to resist, I handed him my key. He went with me into the apartment, told me to stand in the foyer. He put on the lights, looked the place over for intruders, then strode back to where he left me, like a forgotten package.

"Put the chain on after I leave," he instructed. I nodded meekly. He went out the door, closed it halfway, then came back. I was pulling off my hat like a sleepwalker. He tipped up my chin, kissed me firmly, then strode out, slamming the door.

Mechanically I put the chain on and went into the bedroom, pulled off my clothes, scrubbed my hands, and put on my pajamas. A little ticking thought in the back of my mind kept saying, "He kissed me . . . he kissed me." As if it were my first kiss or I needed reminding.

It was still ticking along when I fell into bed and went instantly to sleep.

It wasn't until the next morning that my mind harked back to Bart's comment in the cab, and I realized that he too got around and managed to be Johnny-on-the-spot, as Dad used to say, for not only two crimes, but three.

13. I HAD a number of thoughts when reluctantly I opened my eyes that Wednesday morning. The first was that I should go to sleep again—for the entire day. I hurt all over: my head, my knees, my ego.

Then I remembered the kiss—sharply. After that, all the questions I'd been too beaten down to ask the night before came crowding into my mind. I pulled my aching self out of bed and into the shower. I had to get going if I died on the job—and right then I half wished I would.

But that was only half a wish. Two cups of coffee and I felt stronger, though still discouraged. This was my last day on the case. Hank Deery was due back, and he had a habit of being on time. When I thought of all I had to tell him, I needed more coffee. But as I warned Dawn Ferris, I was going to tell him everything—and that included all I knew about Dr. Wurber, living and dead.

At nine-thirty when I walked in the office, Patsy was at her desk, purring happily. The sight of her reminded me of Dawn and that burned contract, but the kid was so happily confident, it would have been like kicking a kitten to jump on her.

"Oh, Gale, I had a wonderful talk with Miss Ferris

132

yesterday," she announced immediately. Was it only yesterday! It seemed at least ten years ago.

"So I heard," I said, gathering up the mail and a folder Patsy had prepared for me, and heading for my private office.

"Did she leave our copy of the contract with you?" Patsy called after me with a note of confident anxiety. "She said she would."

"She certainly did," I said, noting the ashes still in the tray from Dawn's private fire. I came back to the door between the rooms. "But will you please never, Patsy—not even if we're working on a job for God—let a contract out of your hands?"

"Oh, I wouldn't for anyone else but Miss Ferris," Patsy assured me. "She's different."

I closed the door against the light of such faith, and settled down in the quiet of my own office. Spring sunshine flooded the room, glowed against the beneficent Benson landscape. This day, if ever, I needed peace and clear vision, I thought, as I turned first to the routine matters on my desk.

A few necessary phone calls, a few notes on correspondence, and I finally reached the file Patsy had handed me. My unspoken criticism of the girl melted to full forgiveness. She was a genius at detail.

Here she had assembled, chronologically, the history of Eddie Wells. The material included reports from three credit investigating organizations to which I subscribed, a hotelmen's credit association, and a few police fliers. Each credit association report began with the initial inquiry received by them on Eddie Wells, and there followed, each with its own town and date line, all subsequent reports received on that subject over the years. Thus one report began in 1920 and continued until 1946.

Patsy had cut these dated paragraphs and dovetailed all the reports so that reading down the page I got a complete life story of Eddie Wells. I felt my first lift for the day as I took a cigarette and settled down to study this peculiar case history:

EDWARD CHESTER WELLS, born January 15, 1906, Kansas City, Kansas. Parents deceased.

1920	Kansas City. Arrested for vagrancy. Committed to Home for Wayward Boys. Released 1922. Record good.
1926	Salt Lake City, Utah. Wanted for questioning on a swindle. Last known with Andrews' All Star Carnival.
1927	Portland, Ore. Wanted on charge of forging endorsement two checks, $210. Contact, Matthews, Master Magician, care of AVG or Portland Police.
1927	Seattle, Wash. Due Mrs. Devers' Theatrical Boardinghouse, $180. Last known at liberty. Previously assistant to Matthews, Master Magician.
May 1928	Chicago. Song and dance single. Southside Hotel, bill $88.
July 1928	Atlantic City, N. J. Board bill $36. Did two weeks here in night club on New York Avenue.
Sept. 1928	Philadelphia, Pa. Peter Messaros, tailor, two suits, $90. Holding bad check.
Oct. 1928	Scranton, Pa. Two bad checks, $70.
May 1929	Nashville. Mrs. Evans' guest home, $30.

	Mr. Wells was temporarily embarrassed. Sure he will make full payment as soon as possible.
July 1929	Springfield, Ohio. Bad check, $20. Here with Chautauqua. Smooth talker. No good.
Feb. 1930	Omaha, Neb. Ella Haines, hotel, $78. Stranded here. Nice boy, but vaudeville not doing well. Talking pictures are making things hard for these people.
June 1930	Davenport, Iowa. Flinn, tailor, blue serge suit, white trousers, $65.00. Taught dancing. Snappy-looking fellow, pleasant. No real credit references but took a chance. Skipped.
Oct. 1930	Kansas City, Kansas. Central Hotel. Six weeks' board bill. He sang in the park here this summer. Believe he is in vaudeville now with girl partner, Ethel Waters. Act known as Waters and Wells.

I flipped the long page. This was where I came in, where a new chapter opened and Dawn's story began. I spread the old pictures Patsy had gathered from the theatrical agencies and studied them. Eddie in his white pants and blue coat—the ones for which he did not pay Flinn the tailor. And there was Ethel in her buckety hat, short skirt, and pointy slippers. Would it have made any difference in her future if she could have seen this boy's past history up until the hour she met him? Or could he have charmed her as he charmed Mrs. Evans in Nashville and Miss Haines in Omaha? Eddie had a fetching way, with landladies, tailors—and, on occasion, lovely girls.

The next long page continued this skeleton of a rake's progress. There was detailed evidence of all the heartbreaking petit larceny that had harassed the lovely Dawn in her pre-Dawn days, including an old board bill from Freeport, where Eddie had worked as a singing waiter, and a bad check cashed in New York in June 1933, a month after he and Dawn split the settlement for the baby. Apparently he didn't leave town immediately.

But by that summer's end Eddie's old tour was resumed, highlighted by a paper chase of bad checks and unpaid bills. As I read the next three pages, covering the next ten years, I was amazed that these United States were big enough to furnish him with willing and gullible creditors. Six months here, three months there, six weeks in another place, and always the same story—an unpaid bill and frequently a sympathetic woman.

Then came the three blameless years, 1942-45. Except for one minor charge of drunken driving in Los Angeles, 1944, Eddie Wells, war worker, was behaving himself. I had reached the last page. The sad saga of Eddie picked up again.

Oct. 1945	Los Angeles installment jewelry firm, $120 owing on $250 ring.
Dec. 1945	Los Angeles furrier (time payment plan) $70 owing on a $300 fur jacket.
Jan. 1946	Palm Springs, Calif. Bad check, $140, signed by Edward G. Wells for expenses at hotel for E. C. Wells and wife. Later settled by Cora Mears, also known as Mrs. Edward Wells.

March 1946	San Diego, Calif. Bad check, $80. E. C. Wells and wife. Settled.
April 1946	Los Angeles Music Co. Attachment to reclaim record player purchased by E. C. Wells, Alfredo Hotel. In possession of Cora Mears, 9090 Cohenga Blvd. Title in dispute.
June 1946	Sunset Auto Agency. Car repossessed.
Aug. 1946	E. C. Wells, also known as Ned Wills, arrested on bad-check charge. Case dismissed.
Nov. 1946	Cora Mears, dispossessed, nonpayment of rent, 9090 Cohenga Blvd. Also known as Mrs. Edward Wells. Dispute on responsibility of lessee. Case dismissed.

The last charge against Eddie was that dispossess notice. He could be made to move but not to pay. I read again carefully the record of that last year from the ring bought in 1945 to the apartment out of which they were turned in 1946. Cora—that was what Wurber had called me that night in his office. "You're Cora . . ."

I turned the page. There was one more sheet—the record of Cora Mears. I read it quickly.

Cora Mirowsky, also known as Mears and Wells. Born Pottstown, Pa., 1926. Father: John Mirowsky, miner.

Oct. 1943	Arrested, shoplifting, Wilkes Barre. Suspended sentence. Released in custody of parents.
May 1944	Reported as runaway, located in Chicago.
April 1945	Arrested, Los Angeles, shoplifting. Case

137

	dismissed. Registered with Central Casting. Also bit player, Twentieth Century–Fox.
Aug. 1945	Questioned in bar brawl roundup. Disorderly conduct charge dismissed.
Jan. 1946	Questioned with Edward Wells on bad-check charge, Palm Springs, Calif. Known as Mrs. Edward Wells. Settled.

Somewhere between that brawl in a bar in August and the purchase of a ring on credit in October, Cora had met Wells. For three years, Eddie, getting older, had worked hard and behaved himself, and then Cora came along—lush, greedy, twenty-year-old Cora.

The ring, the coat, the trip to Palm Springs—and in between, the gifts and the meals and the shows and the drinks all presumably paid for out of his war wages. Cora, the reckless kid from Pottstown, who loved pretty things so unwisely that she stole them, became known as Mrs. Eddie Wells. There was no mention of a ceremony. Apparently he was willing for her to have the name, but she wasn't interested in binding herself to a third-rate con man. He'd do until something better came along.

Apparently nothing came. They were evicted from the apartment in her name. That was November. In March or April she was right here in New York with Eddie. Wurber knew about her. "He told me about you . . . I expected a floozie . . ." Wurber was right, but she must have looked like the Queen of Sheba to Eddie. "He liked show," Dawn had said. Cora was glamorous to him, Cora was life. But where was Cora now?

Excitement mounted in me, swift and warm, like a

quick shot of brandy on an empty stomach. Cora could be the answer to everything. She was the link between Eddie Wells's past and the present. She was the one person who might know that Dawn Ferris was Ethel Wells. Eddie would never have missed out on a selling point like that. I could picture him bragging about his ex-wife, trying to impress this girl with the important people he had known. Definitely the person for me to find was Cora Mears.

14. A FRESH plan acted like a shot in the arm. I forgot my aches and bruises as I outlined action for the little time left. I dictated a couple of wires for Patsy to send, gave her a few last-minute instructions, and headed for the elevator. I had just pressed the bell when Patsy came running after me.

"You're wanted on the phone, Gale. It's Mr. Taylor."

"Taylor?"

"Mrs. Alexander's father." My old friend with the walrus mustache and the mean hoe! I went back to the office on the double.

"Remember me?" he asked in that unmistakable voice. When I assured him that I did, he said, "Think maybe I got somethin'."

"Fine! What is it?"

"Now, of course, I can't be sure. I might be sendin' you on a wild-goose chase, if you go at all."

"Don't worry about me. I've chased lots of wild geese. What gives?"

"Maybe I oughtn't 'a' called you. It ain't somethin' I know for sure."

"Mr. Taylor, you impressed me as a man of keen observation. I'd be willing to play along on any hunch you had."

He heaved a great sigh. "I tell you, Miss Gallagher, it does a man good to hear things like that . . . especially when he's lived around here and took what I have to take. No one listenin' to me . . ."

It required several minutes of patient agreement for me to steer him back to the purpose of his call. "Oh, that, yeah. . . . Do you know where Park Place is?"

"Yes. Downtown . . . east of City Hall, near the foot of Brooklyn Bridge."

"Do you know any other Park Place?"

"I think there's one in Brooklyn."

"Nope. This is Manhattan."

"But what is this?" I asked. "Has it something to do with Bette?"

"I don't know," the old man admitted wearily, and my own hopes drooped. "It's an address I got. Like I said, it mightn't have a thing to do with it. But somebody was meetin' there today. I heard it on the telephone extension. Nine-twelve Park Place, Room Ninety."

As I jotted it down, the number looked faintly familiar. "Who was making the date?" I asked.

"I don't know. My hearin' ain't too good—ain't too bad, neither—but it was a man. He was talkin' real low."

"There aren't many men in the Alexander house. When was this?"

"Yesterday morning, around ten o'clock."

"Yesterday. That was shortly before I was out there."

"Everybody was out here," he snapped irritably. "Monty Baxter and that Crane fellow and Wilson, the houseman. Now today there ain't hide nor hair of a soul."

"And Baxter, Wilson, and Crane were all in the house when that call came through?"

"Yup. Could 'a' been any of 'em. I was comin' through the upper hall when the phone rang. I picked it up. Somebody'd already answered downstairs. They talked fast and low, like it was a dark secret. I don't trust one of that bunch."

"Why didn't you tell me this sooner?" I asked.

"I don't exactly trust you, neither. But you did seem to have sense an' I couldn't figure how you could be in on this. You don't even know Sylvia."

"But, Mr. Taylor, you don't mean that your daughter kidnaped her child?"

"No . . . no. It's the no-good people she hangs out with. Now this address, it mightn't be anything."

"I'll take a chance. Thanks for your confidence, Mr. Taylor."

"It's all right," he said gruffly, then added hastily, "Don't let on I told you."

"Not a peep," I promised. "I'll talk to you later."

I replaced the phone as I studied the address, then crossed to the card file, ran through it.

"Patsy, do you remember a case we had last year of the man who deserted his wife in Omaha? He traveled for a toy company."

"That nice Mr. Samuels," Patsy said promptly and sympathetically. "I was so sorry we ever found him for her. He traveled for Tuffy Muff Toys, little fur animals with a muff pocket on back. He gave me one—a blue rabbit. I still have it on my bureau."

As Patsy prattled on, I found the card for the much-married Mr. Samuels. The address was 912 Park Place,

Room 90. I remembered the place very well. If Mr. Samuels was still there he might be helpful. With a few additional instructions to Patsy, I started out again. I would defer my immediate pursuit of Cora Mears for a little side trip to a rookery of strange birds.

There are a number of addresses in Greater New York where all skip tracers call regularly; certain apartment houses, hotels, and office buildings where the fly-by-night congregate with the unerring instinct of homing pigeons. This Park Place building was one of them. It was a very old office building with the open-shaft, cage-type elevator with an operator of the same vintage. An old gentleman wearing a celluloid collar shared the bumpy ride to the ninth floor, which was the top.

Room 90 was one half of the floor. The wall and window space of the huge room was lined with tiny offices, not much bigger than telephone booths. In the center of the room were rows of desks, back to back. By the door, in a small railed-off space, was a switchboard that serviced all these tenants. A directory of the occupants ` hung on the wall above the switchboard.

The din in the room was so terrific I had difficulty in concentrating on the names. The partitions of the little offices were about seven feet high, so that voices rose over them in waves, to mingle with the discussions carried on at the open desks, punctuated by the clatter of business machines. Transactions might be small, but they surely were loud.

After a second review of the tenants, I assured myself that Mr. Samuels was not listed. I turned to the telephone operator, a square, thick-jawed woman who answered all inquiries belligerently. Mr. Samuels was not there any more. Tuffy Muff Toys had no representative there.

I looked over the list again. Most of these people were third-rate sales representatives, but there were some minor individual enterprises, such as a mail-order astrologer, and at the very end a listing that caught my eye—Marty White, advertising. Could that be Marty White, a two-bit bookmaker and numbers man from way back? He had cubicle 11.

The door to the tiny office was ajar, and there, settled comfortably behind the *Racing Form,* was Marty. A dapper little guy in his fifties, he seemed to grow old without ever having grown up. Except for the waxed mustache and the obvious dye job on his black hair, I suspected he hadn't changed much in appearance—or practice—since the days when, according to Dad, Marty matched pennies and cadged butts on Sullivan Street.

"What's good in the fourth?" I asked, pushing open the door. Marty came to his feet with jumping-jack speed, a quick denial on his lips. Then he laughed, grabbed my hand.

"Gale Gallagher! Sit down, beautiful." He swept some old dope sheets off the one other chair, straightened up a pack of cigarettes to offer me a smoke. I'm just naturally a sucker for a warm welcome. I felt better, talking to Marty, while he reminisced about the old days with Dad, but when he mentioned Hank Deery it brought me back to time.

"As a matter of fact, Marty, I'm really down here on a job of work."

144

He preened, twirled his mustache. "Much as I'd like to believe it, Gale, I didn't really think you came down to shoot the breeze with me. But any excuse to see you is a good one. Can I help?"

"I'm not sure, Marty. I don't even know what I'm looking for."

"No matter what it is, you could find it in this dump —if it's no good."

"I suspect it's no good," I agreed. "Marty, notice any new tenants around here lately?"

"Lately? Every day. If some of the pigs out at Jamaica made as good time as these characters, I'd be in the dough."

"This would be someone who looks—different."

He grinned, showing two gold teeth. "Prosperous, huh?"

"I almost said that," I admitted, "but it's not quite what I mean, yet basically it is. Someone with the look of success."

Marty nodded. "I know. I can spot 'em. When I see somebody like that, I try to get next to 'em. Maybe they got a buck or two to kick around."

"Anyone like that lately?"

"A couple of 'em. A guy named Samson from Chicago —says he travels in ties."

From Marty's description, the man sounded as if he traveled in ties. Then there was a fellow selling religious books who evidently got into Room 90 by mistake. I wasn't sure for whom I was looking, but it wasn't those two.

"There's another fellow around here, but he ain't

145

new," Marty said. "Been here six months or a year. I can't tab him. He don't sell anything. He gave me a cold brushoff when I tried to make a pitch. He has good clothes, not too new—like he had lots of good clothes. He's in number twenty-six, down at the end, but he ain't here much. Brock's the name."

"He sounds likely," I said as I rose. "I'll take a look. It's only a shot in the dark—and speaking of shots in the dark, Marty, put this ten on something for me today, will you?"

I shook his dry little hand and returned to the general jungle of Room 90, working my way to the door at the far end. If this man had anything to do with the Alexander kidnaping, he must have been working on the theory that the best place to hide was in a crowd. But he wasn't hiding there that morning. The door was closed and locked and there was no light behind the partition.

I glanced at my watch. It was almost eleven. The morning was getting away and I had a lot to do. This might be one of those things where you waited two weeks for someone to show. I went back to the glum-faced operator and asked if she knew when Mr. Brock would be in.

"Mr. Brock!" The name practically did a face-lifting job for her. "He doesn't come in every day. He's a gentleman with many interests."

"Could you name a few?" I asked, leaning on the rail between us and holding out my wallet, so she could see the identification. She spluttered.

"I'm sure Mr. Brock never . . ."

"It's merely a double check on a friend of his," I assured her, and she puffed down to a stop. But she wiggled her bulk on the swivel chair, like an outsized hen, patted her upsweep and answered three calls on the board before she came back to me.

"Mr. Brock is an investment broker. He's got other offices. He only uses this for some personal affairs." She actually beamed. "I think it's philanthropy."

I didn't like that bemused look of hers. Somebody had been turning on the charm, but big. The only charmer I'd found on the case was Bart Crane, and I was afraid I was finding him too often.

"You expect Mr. Brock today?" I asked.

"I never know when to expect him. Sometimes he comes in every day for a while, then doesn't show up for weeks. I haven't seen him in ten days." Then very solemnly she added, "He's a very fine man."

It was a recommendation from the heart—a heart that apparently didn't get much exercise. I stood by, thoughtfully pulling on my gloves, while she gruffly answered two phone calls, screamed at a tenant, and snapped rudely at the postman. This Brock really had her doing ground loops, when the mere mention of his name made her agreeable. In the next lull I stepped to the rail to thank her. She looked up, then suddenly her gaze fixed somewhere beyond my shoulder. The glow in her eyes was comparable only to a Pacific sunset.

"There's Mr. Brock now!" she said.

I turned slowly, reluctantly, with a touch of icy dread in my middle. In the next moment, I don't know which of us was the most surprised, myself—or Montgomery

Baxter. Certainly I recovered first and managed to control a wild desire to laugh at the pompous Baxter in the role of charmer.

"This lady was looking for you, Mr. Brock," the operator said in honeyed tones.

"I'm so glad I caught you, Mr. Brock," I said, with emphasis on the name, but from his expression it was the verb that struck home.

With a nod, Baxter strode off to cave 26 with me right on his heels. The back of his neck was scarlet and his rather thick shoulders were humped with fury. His hand shook as he put the key in the lock, banged open the door. This office was exactly like Marty's, except that it was neatly kept. There was nothing in sight but the locked roll-top desk and two chairs.

Baxter switched on the light, put his hat and coat on a wall peg. Enjoying myself for a moment, I took the chair by the side of the desk, lighted a cigarette. He sat at the locked desk, facing me. His present anger and the strain of the past week combined to give his face a puffed, bloated look. I thought he really should watch his blood pressure.

"What do you want?" he asked, his voice too reflecting the strain.

"My mission hasn't changed since yesterday," I said. "I merely thought that the occupant of this office might throw some new light on it."

"This is my private office. It has nothing to do with Bette Alexander," he said in a grating whisper. "How did you find it?"

"I merely walked in and there it was," I said flip-

148

pantly. "Do the police or the FBI know about this little business nest? They usually ask rather personal questions of all concerned when there has been a kidnaping."

"They didn't discover it, Miss Gallagher," he said, mopping his round face. "There was no reason why I should tell them. It has nothing whatever to do with the case."

The operator had said he hadn't been around in ten days. Obviously he was taking no chances in leading a possible shadow to this place. But today he had to come, regardless of chances. To meet that person with whom he'd talked on the phone?

"Mr. Baxter, I too am working with the police. My entire dossier on this case is to be given them in twenty-four hours. I won't conceal anything I've turned up, unless I am convinced it has nothing to do with the case."

His blood pressure visibly dropped a couple of points as I went on. "I do know that sometimes persons innocently connected with such cases as the Alexander kidnaping receive publicity that wrecks their lives." I let that sink in, then added, "I have no wish to cause undue hardship—but I have to have facts."

"You are a very remarkable young woman, Miss Gallagher," he said earnestly. He was turning on the charm that got the telephone operator. It belonged to the "look straight in the eye and speak low" school of hypnosis.

"You have summed up the situation most astutely. My maintaining this office has nothing whatever to do with the Alexander case, but the revelation of it could cause me great personal inconvenience. I have had the office for many months. You can confirm that right here."

I already knew it from Marty White, but I said nothing, let him continue.

"Miss Gallagher, I was forced to take this office. While my connection with *the family* has always been most agreeable, there are times when it does become too absorbing. I have no life—no business of my own. I have to live and think and breathe for the Alexander family."

"I can see that might be oppressive," I said. He nodded grimly, stopped to light a cigarette. His hand was still not steady.

"There are times when—if you'll pardon me—it is plain hell." He leaned forward, punctuating his remarks with a stubby finger. "There is not only Mrs. Alexander to be pleased, but the three executors of the estate, the head of the Alexander Realty Corporation, who manages the properties, the president of the bank, and a doctor who was Theodore Alexander's closest friend. All these people have things to say, advice that must be listened to, if not taken. . . ." His voice rose, until he remembered the low partitions; then he cut it down abruptly.

"Altogether it is very trying. So I took this little office, cheap but private." He bristled. "Do you know that I don't have a desk in the Alexander home or in their uptown office that is my own?"

I could only sympathize with the man. I wouldn't have such a job for the entire Alexander fortune. I could certainly see the reasonableness of his claim. I thought I could also see the faint shadow of larceny.

"I'm sorry that I, too, had to intrude on your hard-won privacy, Mr.—Brock," I said, smiling. Then I glanced helplessly at the smoldering butt of a cigarette in my fingers. I'd been flicking ashes on the floor, but this . . .

With a flutter of apologies, he pulled out his keys, started to open the roll-top desk. Then suddenly he turned and pushed the metal waste basket toward me.

"Drop it here. You'll burn yourself," he said. Whatever was in the desk, he was taking no chances on giving me a look-see. I tossed the butt away and rose.

We shook hands, parted with no promises. He asked for none, I made none. I got a farewell smile from the operator, whose day was made now that Mr. Brock had arrived. Slowly I walked down the wide hall, which really was a huge balcony or gallery squaring off around the open cage of the elevators. I hesitated for a moment at the elevator door, then continued around the hall to the opposite side. Despite the interference of columns and grillework, I could see the entrance to Room 90.

On the door of 97 a battered card read: "Back at one." I lounged against a column facing the door. From there I could watch the traffic coming and going into Room 90.

My wait was brief. Not five minutes later, Baxter himself came hurrying down the hall, entered the elevator. Apparently the tryst was called off. I waited another five minutes, then I too took the elevator and held my breath as it descended, creaking, to the street floor.

Out of the clouds of suspicion in my mind, I was pulling another plan.

15.

I WAS still thinking over angles of this new idea after I'd made two phone calls and caught an express to Brooklyn. It was a good hour for subway travel to Flatbush. The train was half empty—a few early shoppers homeward bound, a girl struggling with a young baby and a zipper bag, probably headed for a visit with Mother, an insurance man making up his book as he rode, two ladies en route to a bridge luncheon. I'd never been to a bridge luncheon. . . .

My mind came back from its suburban excursion. There was that idea about Montgomery Baxter, alias Mr. Brock. A little larceny is a dangerous thing. There were a number of ways in which Baxter might get away with minor larceny: a commission on purchases made for the Alexander estate, a "bonus" for influence, a straight cut on overcharging. They were the familiar ones, and he didn't impress me as being especially original.

But an extra thousand or two can spread a budget, spread it to include little luxuries that are hard to eliminate. People spoil so easily. I knew—as Dad always insisted—that little crimes lead to big ones. If Baxter had reason for petit larceny, he might find a reason, or

152

at least a need, for a bigger take or a bigger risk—like kidnaping.

Somewhere out beyond Ebbets Field I changed to a local, and two stations later came up out of the cut through which the trains run at that point into a wide pleasant business street. It was high noon. Children were coming out of school—streams of comfortably dressed, well-fed children. They ebbed around me as I walked, dropping away a few at a time, into apartment houses, private homes, cross streets.

A few of them were still with me when I reached Corley Road. It is a very pretty street with stone houses separated by driveways and fronted with small lawns, green in that early spring. An occasional forsythia bush gleamed like blossoming sunshine while crocuses edged some of the walks. The trees on the curbside were in bud.

The street gave me a pang. I hadn't been in this part of Brooklyn for so long. But years ago Dad and I used to walk out here on his day off. These houses were new then, back around 1928, and once we looked at a "sample" house.

"Someday, Gale," he said, "we'll have a house like this. You know Gramma wouldn't be happy away from the old neighborhood and the old parish, but we won't always have her with us. We can wait. When the time comes, we'll have a house like this."

A house like the one at 825 Corley Road, with the name of Baxter on the mailbox. I pressed the bell. Chimes sounded. A moment later the door opened and a small trim woman with light brown hair and a neat rayon print said, "Yes?"

153

"Mrs. Baxter?"

She repeated the yes in a different key. "I'm from the Associated Newspapers," I said quickly. "I'm doing a human interest story on Bette Alexander. I'd like to talk to you about her."

She took a step backward, shaking her head. "I don't know anything about it. You'd have to see my husband."

"We have seen your husband—many times. We won't quote you, if you don't wish us to, but—you do know Bette Alexander, don't you?"

"Of course, I've met the child. In fact, she's often been here. My daughters have played with her, but my husband particularly. . . ."

I smiled at her reassuringly. "That is why this angle of the story has not been told. We want another mother's picture of this child." I talked fast, in sort of a sentimental coax. In a couple of minutes I was sitting in the living room.

It was a nice room, a bit too precise, a bit too colorless, but still a nice room, just as Mrs. Baxter was a nice woman, with the same modifications. She had lovely hands and feet and was rather pretty except for a small but deep line between her brows. It might have indicated the need of eyeglasses or the presence of some chronic frustration. A certain nervousness in her manner I guessed to be new.

"I simply don't know where I am these days," she said, sitting on the edge of an overstuffed chair. "We've been so upset ever since Bette was taken. You can imagine how my husband is."

"I've seen him," I said.

"But you really have no idea. He hasn't been home.

Well, he hasn't had a good night's sleep since it happened. None of us have, really."

"You have daughters?" I inquired.

"Yes, two. Doris and Edna." She gave a proud little nod toward a silver-framed picture on an end table. The picture was taken some time ago, judging from the clothes, and showed Mrs. Baxter with two girls, about ten and twelve. The children were average, pleasant-looking kids. It was Mrs. Baxter who fascinated me. She hadn't aged at all; even the deep little worry line between her brows was there then.

"This apparently is not a recent picture, and yet—you really look younger today."

She flushed and fluttered at what was undoubtedly a familiar compliment. "That was taken ten years ago," she admitted. "The year Doris—she's the eldest—finished grade school. Now they're both graduated from high and have excellent positions. Edna is engaged."

"You don't look old enough to have a grown family, Mrs. Baxter," I said honestly.

"I am forty-seven," she admitted, almost happily. But then, they were happy years to which she was admitting, contented, protected years in this house, with this family. The Baxters lived well but not extravagantly. The girls were self-supporting. Nothing to indicate a reason for larceny.

"Now about Bette Alexander . . ." I prompted.

Relaxed, Mrs. Baxter warmed up to the subject quickly. "Bette is a darling. Unlike all the things I've heard of other wealthy children, she is completely unspoiled. She liked to stay with us overnight, and she'd say, 'Aunt Edna'—she always called me Aunt Edna—

'Aunt Edna, may I run the vacuum cleaner in the morning?' She thought that was a treat, she really did.''

"Bette must have been quite devoted to your husband, having known him all her life."

"Oh, yes, of course," Mrs. Baxter agreed flatly. She herself noticed the change of tone and laughed apologetically. "My husband is very fond of Bette, but he's just not good with children. As he always said, the girls and the home were my department, and the finances were his."

Edna Baxter was wound up by that time, and with very little encouragement talked on about Bette and her girls—how Bette stayed with them when Theodore Alexander died, and how she took Bette and the girls to the seashore for a month in the first year of the war.

While I half listened, I was trying to put facts together and come up with an answer. But nothing added. Montgomery Baxter and his wife went together as perfectly as ham and eggs. Obviously same type, same background, and with temperaments that complemented each other. She had a kinder, warmer personality than he, but she also had a certain childish quality, common in many emotionally retarded if not actually frigid women. I suspected that the Baxters had twin beds or separate rooms, and that she confided to her friends that they were "through with that sort of thing."

Baxter—the charmer of telephone operators—would probably be resigned to that arrangement and might accept it as something to be expected in a good woman. Plainly Edna Baxter was a very good woman. I liked her and felt a little sorry for her. With half a chance, I thought, she might have been an even better woman.

156

I made a few notes in a little leather-bound memo pad I carried, to give an air of authenticity to the interview. There were several other items on the pad—the Park Place address and the name of Brock, which I was sure Edna Baxter had never heard. The trail of Old Man Taylor's wild-goose chase. That's what it was.

Just as I told Bart Crane, everybody had fish to fry. Something to hide, something personal to save, something to louse up the case. Nobody really telling the truth. Sylvia Alexander had been tied up with Wurber. There was something crooked in that, but I didn't want to remember Wurber.

Now Baxter had his own little game of put and take. After reviewing the domestic situation, it looked very small. I was sure the police and the FBI had gone through his past and present with a fine-tooth comb. The manipulations of Mr. Brock had escaped only because they were so small.

I closed my notebook, dropped it in my pocket, prepared to leave. I thanked Edna Baxter for her help, and she rose beaming.

"It's been a real pleasure, Miss . . ."

"Grossinger," I said, remembering a wonderful week end at that famous resort and the G embroidered on my blouse that might be visible.

"Miss Grossinger," Mrs. Baxter echoed, in her obedient-little-girl tone. "You make interviewing a real pleasure. You are so understanding. Of course, you won't quote me—that is, direct?"

"You have my word."

We were moving toward the door, which opened, without benefit of foyer, from the living room to the

157

street. She was saying, "Mr. Baxter says you can't trust the press. They twist everything you say—to make it dramatic, that is."

"He has handled the press very well. He has had a big job."

Her hand was on the doorknob. "You have no idea," she said. "He's a nervous wreck. He really is, and I always said he had no nerves. He's spent only one night home since it happened. And before that—well, it is March and income tax. Why people so rich should wait so long . . ."

"I thought that was only me," I said, grinning.

"The withholding system does help, don't you think?" she asked brightly. I couldn't explain that I had my own business, so I merely nodded.

"And it's not only the tax," Edna Baxter continued, nursing the doorknob. "So many things. Wealthy people really are very inconsiderate. I suppose it's because they have so much. Last week, for instance—that is, right before Bette was taken—Mr. Baxter had conferences every night with one of the coexecutors at the Phrygian Club."

"The what?"

"Phrygian Club. It's very exclusive. One of those things where you have to be put in by an ancestor or something. I don't really understand it. Anyway, it's a Murray Hill exchange. You see, it was the week that Edna's engagement was to be announced. So many things came up, I just had to know where to reach Mr. Baxter. Well, I was just trying to show you what I mean—so many demands."

"I understand perfectly," I said, "and thanks so much."

The children were going back to school, so that I seemed to pick up the wave again as I walked back to the subway. I watched for a drugstore I'd spotted en route to the Baxters', and made for the telephone booth. I dialed Eve Craig, an old friend of mine who was editor of a club directory.

"What do you know about the Phrygian Club?" I asked.

"You would want to know just as I'm about to go out to lunch. It's a snooty outfit, started by some precious old boys back in the eighties. It's the kind where they enroll the kids the day they're born—the boys. It's all male."

"Could you get me the membership?"

"Got it on file."

"I'll be over in forty minutes."

"My secretary will take care of you. I'll tell her to have the list waiting."

I called Patsy then and got the names of the coexecutors of the Alexander estate from our files. They had been listed in the newspaper accounts. She had nothing new to report and there had been no replies to my wires. After that I only stopped long enough for a cup of coffee.

Forty minutes later, on the nose, I walked into the office of the Craig Club Directory on Lexington Avenue. Eve Craig's secretary was waiting for me. She handed me the list and showed me into a private office to study it.

It wasn't very long, this list limited to children of members. The names spelled out New York history. Quickly I searched for the three co-executors. Not one was a member of the Phrygians. It had to be this club because Edna Baxter had telephoned her husband there.

I started at the top, looking for a lead. The masthead gave me the first surprise. It was a name listed among the eight founders—Theodore Alexander. That would be the first Theodore Alexander, Bette's grandfather. His son would also have been a member, but he was dead.

My eye ran down the list of names, and then I had the second surprise. The name leaped at me like something alive—John Bartley Crane. He was back again. But why was he meeting Monty Baxter every night in that week before Bette's kidnaping? Why did he keep appearing? And why was I so afraid to ask?

16. AS I walked along Lexington Avenue, I felt as though I'd just got off a merry-go-round, a long ride and no brass rings. I was right back where I started from, three hours earlier, if not three days earlier. Certainly the morning added up to nothing. So Baxter was a two-bit cheat. So what?

There were a few things, such as those conferences between Baxter and Bart Crane in the days before the kidnaping. I had patches of knowledge about those days, but not enough to make a quilt. It was during that time that Eddie Wells wrote to Dawn, that Wurber and Eddie met, that Eddie talked to Wurber about Cora. I was back to her again.

Wearily I headed for the Third Avenue El, rode to the station nearest Eddie's last address. The street looked less formidable in the daylight, but it was a depressing contrast to Corley Road. The contrast was most marked in the miserable-looking children playing on the sidewalk in dusty bars of sunshine that filtered down through the perpetual shadow of the El track. Mothers rocked baby carriages, sat in doorways, or shouted down from upper windows. I wondered why, with all the pleasant inexpensive places to live in these United States, poor people stayed in this most expensive of cities. Didn't they have the courage to go, or like myself, did they just love New York?

At the doorway to that dreary house, a slatternly young mother of twins casually watched her offspring while she read a pulp love magazine. She glanced at me curiously as I entered the grimy vestibule, continued purposefully through the dirty hall to the rear apartment from which the landlady had come that night. I heard voices and sharp laughter. I had to knock twice before the big woman with the missing teeth opened the door. She remembered me at once, but obviously didn't like the recollection.

"Oh, you come to see Mr. Wells. The police . . . "

"I've spoken to them about it," I said quickly. "Have they been here today?"

She shook her head, her eyes clouded with suspicion. I went on in my most pleasant tone. "It's very important that I talk to you, Mrs. . . . "

"Petrucci," she murmured reluctantly. "I talk police. No one else."

"But I am with the police." I flashed my identification card, which she undoubtedly couldn't read, but it must have looked official. She visibly weakened.

"You liked Mr. Wells, Mrs. Petrucci," I persisted. "You don't want his murderer to go unpunished."

She lifted her fat shoulders as if murderers were no concern of hers, but she did let me into an incredibly stuffy room. In the kitchen beyond three women sat at a table drinking beer and pointedly ignoring us.

"Mr. Wells was a nice man," I continued. "He never wanted to hurt anyone. You liked him."

162

Mrs. Petrucci's dark eyes darted toward her beer drinking friends and she nodded. "He was good. Buy beer, drink one." Her big bosom heaved regretfully.

"You'd known him a long time?"

"No." She rubbed a dirt-crusted knuckle thoughtfully against a work-hardened palm—though from the looks of the place, she couldn't have got those calluses there. "Mebbe two, three week." Her face brightened. "Three week Friday. Willie he go, Mr. Wells come. Seem longer."

"How much did he owe you?"

"He pay good!" Ella Haines of Omaha should have heard that. "He got big money soon. I tell cops Mr. Wells got rich friends."

"Like that blonde girl? Did she ever come back?" Mrs. Petrucci shook her head, never using a word when a gesture would serve the purpose.

"What did she look like, Mrs. Petrucci? Was she my size . . . taller, slimmer?"

Mrs. P. really went to town with the gestures then, making a sketch in the air of a tall curvy girl. "And her hair—she shine," she finished, while I did some quick totaling.

Dawn's hair shone and she had curves, but she was smaller than I. Sylvia Alexander was blonde and curvaceous—and tall.

"Have you ever seen her—this blonde girl—here anytime before the day Mr. Wells died?" Mrs. Petrucci had relaxed now and was beginning to enjoy the importance of her role.

"One time I see her late at night. And such fine

furs . . . " She gave a caressing little moan. "She come downstairs fast, like she mad to hell. She went with man in a big car. Rich people!"

Busy people, I thought, up to no good. "And what about a girl with auburn—red hair?"

She laughed, shrugged. "He liked da blonde girls."

I tried several angles but Mrs. Petrucci knew only what she saw. She didn't know where Eddie had lived before he came here, she didn't know if he got any mail. To men visitors she paid no heed. I gave her a bill to buy some beer for her friends, thanked her, and left.

Obviously Cora wasn't with Eddie when he came to Mrs. Petrucci's house, three weeks earlier. But she was in New York. Wurber knew about her. And he had been to see Eddie at the "hole," as he called the flat, the day before Bette was kidnaped. Four days earlier, Eddie had written Dawn implying that their child was in danger.

For several weeks this thing had been planned. Eddie knew about it, so did Wurber, so did the tall blonde who left Eddie's room "mad to hell." Could that have been Sylvia? Who was the man in the car? And would she deliberately put an innocent youngster in such jeopardy —such double danger?

I was walking south on Third Avenue when the familiar phrase echoed in my mind. At the same time I realized I was at the corner where Bart Crane caught up with me on Monday night. I'd been trying not to think about Bart, but it wasn't easy. There were too many questions about him that I didn't want to ask, though, I told myself irritably, I didn't see where pussyfooting was going to get me.

Bart had every opportunity of being in on this thing

from the start. He knew Bette and Sylvia. He met with Baxter at the Phrygian Club, though he obviously was a welcome visitor at the Alexander home. He seemed to be acting as contact man and denied knowing either Eddie or Wurber, but he was awfully close by when those two turned up dead. When, even in my bewildered state, I tried to ask questions the previous evening, he had brushed me off. Noah Taylor kept shouting it was an inside job. Maybe he had something. Maybe he had a lot.

This, I thought savagely, walking faster, was not getting me any closer to Cora, and time was running out. It was past two. I thought of dropping over to Dario's bar. That was a top favorite in hangouts for that area, and there was a big chance that Eddie—a barfly from way back—would have found the place by instinct and at some time taken Cora in there. But Mike Nash didn't come on duty until four o'clock, so that question would have to wait.

I went down to 86th Street and called the office, but the phone was busy. I had a chocolate malted milk while I waited and called it lunch. I got Patsy on the second try.

"Oh, Gale, I just got the wire from Pottstown. Western Union have the cutest fellows now. Remember during the war how they used to have old ladies and kids . . . "

"Never mind their personnel. Read me the message."

"I was coming to that. I got it right here." A sprightly whistled tune and the rustle of paper came over the phone; then Patsy was back with her official telephone voice—entirely different from her normal tone. It rather suggested a long-distance operator suddenly gone high hat.

"The message re-ads," Patsy chanted, "Cora Mirowsky, also known as Mears, in town three days during Christmas week. Last address Nine-fifty West Seventieth Street, New York City. Present occupation unknown. Record here clear at present." Patsy slid back to a conversational tone. "That address what you want, Gale?"

"That's it," I said. "I'll call you later."

"Shall I wait?"

"Not after five. This may be a busy day."

I was making plans as I came out of the drugstore and the headline for which I'd been waiting all day caught my eye: "Doctor Found Murdered." I bought the paper, folded it casually under my arm, and tried to get a cab. It seemed a medium-sized eternity before a taxi finally picked me up and got me off the street before a patrol car did it. By this time, the police must be looking for me.

I told the driver to drop me at 72nd and West End Avenue, which would be near enough, then turned with studied calm to the paper . . . and the account of Dr. Wurber's death.

"The body of Dr. Alois Wurber was found in the unfurnished living room of his former residence on West 66th street by Patrolman George Williams at an early hour this morning. The doctor had been shot in the throat and chest, apparently at close range. No weapon was found."

The story continued with a detailed report, given by neighbors, of strange noises heard in the empty house. These included angry voices, heavy footsteps, a woman's scream—that was me—and insistent ringing of the bell. They got the time confused with the performance of the drunken woman across the street, but one neighbor came through with a straight item. She had seen a tall man with a slight limp and a woman of medium height leave the doctor's house at one-thirty. Police were seeking this couple for questioning, which, I reflected, after reading the concluding paragraph of the story, would be only a matter of minutes now.

"Dr. Wurber," the account continued, "who owned and occupied the house for many years and at one time conducted a small maternity hospital there, moved only yesterday to his new place in Shortridge, New Jersey, where he planned to devote all his time to a convalescent home he recently established. Reputed to be of Austrian birth, the doctor was fifty-four years old and unmarried."

I folded the paper, creased it carefully with cold hands. It was almost three o'clock. Hank Deery would be back on duty at four. He knew I was with Wurber when I found Eddie's body. He would connect the cases immediately, and once they got on the trail of Wurber, it would lead to the Alexander case. But before that, I was sure it would lead to me. Hank would never wait for tomorrow morning now. He'd get to me as fast as he could . . . which would be very fast.

"Which corner, lady?" the driver asked. I roused myself, realized we were almost at West End Avenue.

I said the nearest corner would do, paid him off, then walked quickly south to 70th and into the dead-end block that stopped against the bulwark of the West Side Express Highway edging the Hudson River. A mixed

167

neighborhood, it was a big improvement over the dingy environs of Third Avenue. As on many Manhattan streets, smart residences elbowed dreary rooming houses, brownstone fronts trimly converted to apartments were shoulder to shoulder with tenements.

The address I wanted was far down the block and about midway in the scale of appearances. A small sign reading "Furnished Rooms—Light Housekeeping" had a "No Vacancy" sign across its face. I rang the bell marked "Miley, Supt."

A teen-age girl answered my ring. She wore her black hair in an enormous pompadour, a peasant-type blouse with a neckline wide as an escape hatch, no stockings, and red sandals. She looked as if she were practicing to be a tart.

"We don't have any vacancies," she said rudely as she opened the door a few inches, using the red-sandaled foot as a doorstop.

"I'm not looking for a room. I wanted to inquire about a former tenant of yours."

"Mamma's out," she said quickly. "You'll have to come back at six."

I managed to edge into the narrow opening of the door, glimpsed a boy of her own age lounging on a bench in the hall, who was no doubt the reason for her haste.

"This couple, Miss Miley . . . you are Miss Miley? You might remember them. They came from Hollywood."

Her eyes widened. "Oh, you mean Cora? She moved weeks ago." She leaned against the door frame, regarding me with new interest. "You a friend of hers?"

"I'm a friend of a friend of hers. We're trying to locate her."

"She moved over on the east side somewhere. She didn't leave no address but she promised to call me, and if she does . . ."

"Are *you* a friend of hers?" I asked.

"Sort of. She's been in pictures and now she's looking for a stage play. She says that's the best way to get discovered." The boy friend was forgotten.

"Are you in the theater, Miss Miley?" I asked gravely. Her rather unpleasant blue eyes got wider than campaign buttons and under the lolling blouse her bra was straining at its hooks.

"Oh, no, not yet; but Cora says I got real talent."

"It's obvious. It's very important that I get in touch with Cora. If you could tell me a little more about her, help me find her, then we could all get together, discuss her plans and yours."

She swung the door wide. "Come in," she said, and to the boy, "Go'n wait in the kitchen, Lester. I gotta talk to this lady."

In five minutes I knew the history of Tess Miley, including her parents' divorce, her mother's problems as the operator of several furnished-room houses, and her efforts to make seventeen-year-old Tess finish high school. I listened another five minutes to a recitation of her burning desire to be an actress. It wasn't an ambition; she didn't want to work for it. She merely wanted it to happen.

"Cora says it's all in meeting the right people. Look at Lauren Bacall."

"Has Cora some good contacts lined up?"

"Terrific. You know, she's sultry. I wish I could be sultry. It really gets the men."

"Isn't Cora married?"

Tess darted me a questioning glance. "Well, I guess so—sort of. That's one reason Mamma wanted her to move. Mamma's a very particular woman about who she has in her houses, and she thought Cora gave me ideas."

"I doubt it," I said, and Tess beamed.

"Mr. Wells is old—forty at least, and while he *is* kind of cute, he's not glamorous. He hasn't lived."

That, too, was open to doubt, but as it was too late to do anything about it anyway, I made no comment. Tess continued in a whisper, "I think Cora's going to leave him. She's got a rich man with a beautiful car."

I had a vision of Bart Crane's slick gray convertible in the drive at the Alexander house. "What color is the car?" I asked.

"Light. I only saw it once, at night. She met him while she was here, and I think she and Ed split up when they left."

"Just when was that, Tess?"

"I don't know." She frowned. Time was as vague to her as it was to Mrs. Petrucci. "Oh, sure, I know—three weeks ago Friday. Because Lester and I went to the Paramount and stayed for two shows. She was gone when I got home."

"Did Cora register with any theatrical agents while she was here? If she was going on the stage . . ."

"She was planning on that, but she went down to Pottstown to spend Christmas with her folks, and when she came back, she was just getting ready for her career when she met this other fellow—and everything changed."

"Who is he? He sounds very important."

"I guess he is, but she didn't tell me his name. She just called him Buzzy." Tess scowled, dug her toe into the worn hall carpet. "I don't think it's so awful to be kept."

"It's a precarious livelihood," I said. "Do you think Cora was going to make a career of it?"

"She could—she was so glamorous and sultry."

"Redheads can give that effect," I said.

"Redheads . . . yeah, like Rita Hayworth. Oh—you meant Cora?" Tess laughed. "Didn't you know? She's not a redhead any more. She got a terrific dye job in March. She's a blonde now."

17.

I WAS almost as excited as Patsy at her best when I found a telephone and dialed the office. One thought was spinning through my mind—Cora was a blonde.

This might change everything, explain everything. For a moment another thought flickered, a glimpse of something half remembered, but Patsy answered the phone then and the shadowy thought eluded me.

Immediately Patsy said: "Lieutenant Deery from Homicide called you. He said it was important."

"If he calls again, forget you talked to me. Better still, close the office early today. Now give me Dawn Ferris's home phone number."

"You sound awful cheery, Gale. Did something happen?"

"I think it's about to happen. I'll tell you later."

"But do you mean I should go home now—at four o'clock?"

"Believe me, it's for the good of the business."

I left Patsy bubbling like a teakettle when I cut the connection and called Dawn Ferris. A cool-voiced maid answered. I tried to match her calm but I was jittery. I was sure Dawn wouldn't want to talk to me and I had to see her. I was surprised when Dawn answered with

172

that velvet voice that pours into the ears of millions of housewives twice every day.

"I must see you, Dawn, right away. It's a matter of life and death—and I don't mean ours."

She didn't reply for a second; then, "I only this moment got in from the studio. I'm so tired, Gale. Of course, if I really thought I could help . . ."

My spirits got a quick lift. "You can, and we have so little time. I'm coming up to see you at once. I only wanted to be sure you were at home."

"I'm home," she said flatly, but I didn't need encouragement. Tess Miley had given me more hope than I ever expected to find, more than enough to carry me ahead, now that Dawn would co-operate even a little.

Ten minutes later the quiet-voiced mulatto maid, who might have come right out of a play, showed me into Dawn's living room—which might have come out of a play, too. It was a beautiful room, all done in soft blues and grays, dominated by a painting of jungle scene rich with exciting greens. It made a dramatic vis-à-vis to the picture window at the opposite side of the room that framed a view of the East River.

Despite its dramatic effectiveness, the room was surprisingly homelike, comfortable, and relaxing. I found myself breathing more easily as I crossed the soft carpet, so lush it had a cuddly quality to it. A photograph on the piano arrested my progress. It was the picture of a man—not handsome but strong, a clear-eyed man with tremendous vitality and assurance. Here was a person whose word could be depended upon, whose actions were sure, but who might be longer on justice than mercy.

"You like him?" I glanced around. I hadn't heard Dawn as she crossed the room, so beautiful in this her own special setting that I almost gasped with delight.

I often wonder if beautiful people know the pleasure they give others. Certainly Dawn seemed unaware of it, which was half her charm. It was the first time I ever saw her without a hat. She wore her hair dressed simply, brushed back from her low forehead in a chignon on her neck. The blue hostess gown was long-sleeved and trailing, her only jewelry a large sapphire ring. I wished I could have shown her as an exquisite model to Tess Miley.

"I really was tired," she said, half in apology, "so I changed. I've asked Leila to bring cocktails." As she spoke she moved the picture on the piano slightly, with a gesture that was a caress. "You do like him?"

"Geoffrey Wilton?" She nodded. "He's very interesting-looking, but I'd say he'd stand no nonsense."

"Yes, he's like that . . . forthright to a fault." Her eyes were thoughtful. "He's been away two weeks. I only hope before he comes back . . ."

She wasn't kidding about being tired. Weariness drew fine spider lines around her eyes, gave that pulled look to her throat I'd noticed once before. But in spite of everything, I still liked her very much. There was a gallant quality about her that appealed to me even more than her beauty.

I said, "Have you seen the papers?"

"No, I only just came in." She glanced at me quickly. "Is there more about—Eddie?"

"It's Wurber this time, Dawn." I handed her the paper. She read it walking away from me, but her shoulders were tight, her elbows close to her sides as if it took a physical effort to control herself. She made a soft whimpering sound that was almost a moan. Yet as the maid entered, wheeling a portable bar, Dawn turned, managed a smile, and thanked the girl.

I took a chair facing Dawn, as she poured me a Manhattan, offered me a selection of tiny sandwiches; every inch the perfect hostess, though her mind must have been seething. She took two sips of her drink before she spoke. "Was it this—about Wurber—that you wanted to tell me? Was this what you meant about life and death?"

"I was talking of Bette. I'm sure now that Eddie knew about her. It was this kidnaping plan that he referred to in the letter."

"Oh, I know it! I know it!" Dawn cried desperately. "It's haunted me night and day, Gale. If only I'd gone to meet him . . ."

"Don't start tormenting yourself with that. Eddie had played 'Wolf, wolf!' too many times to be trusted. How could you know this was the truth?"

"If only there were something I could do . . ."

"There is," I cut in. "You can come clean with me. Who scared you off this case?"

The masked look came back in her eyes, her voice went cool. "I can't tell you," she said, then faltered, her defenses crumbling. "I don't even know. I'm not sure if the voice belonged to a man or a woman, but it said if I wanted to save her, I had to get out . . . stay out . . . And you see what's happened, Gale . . . to Eddie . . . to Wurber."

"I see, all right. But any minute now I'm going to be off the case and the police are going to be in it—all

175

over it—with angles they haven't had until now. I can't hold out any longer."

Dawn glanced at me shrewdly. "You were the girl who was seen leaving Wurber's house last night? You were there too?"

I nodded. "Wurber came to see me—to scare me off. I had a hunch that he had Bette in his house. I was wrong. The house was empty—except for him."

"And the other man?"

"John Bartley Crane, the artist."

"He did Bette's picture," Dawn said eagerly. "That darling picture in the riding habit."

"According to his account, he's very fond of her."

"Did he go there with you?" Dawn asked. I told her then what had happened. It eased me to talk about it, and what was there to lose now? Dawn listened, fascinated.

"But the word on the floor, Gale, G-o-r . . . What does it mean?"

"That's what I hoped you could tell me. The name of the person who threatened you, perhaps."

She shook her head. "I wouldn't know. Oh, I'd tell you now, if I did." She sprang up, paced the floor. "I've waited as long as I can humanly endure it. We've got to get that child if we can. I don't care who she belongs to."

"Then when I tell the police tonight and the story breaks . . ."

"I don't care. I'll telephone Geoff tonight in San Francisco. It's hard to explain such a thing over the wire, but he has to hear it from me. After that—I don't care."

176

"There's a girl, too," I said as Dawn stopped at the bar, poured fresh cocktails. "Eddie's girl, Cora Mears." I told Dawn about her, the redhead who was now a blonde. "If it was Cora, she was described as beautiful by the landlady, as sultry by dizzy little Tess Miley, sufficiently good-looking to do bit parts in pictures, and finally to attract a rich man—also according to Tess Miley."

Dawn's eyes were shining. "But Cora! The name, Gale! Did you think of that? Could Wurber have been writing her name?"

"I thought of it all right, but his handwriting is in a clear unmistakable script. He made the old-fashioned vertical G with the looped tail—even in his death throes he was a precisionist."

"But if Cora is involved in the case, as you think, who is this rich man? The one with the car?"

I hesitated. "It could be Bart Crane. He has a new car. He's very charming—deadly charming. He evidently won Bette's confidence, which would be necessary for such a kidnaping. I believe she went with someone she knew. He also has Sylvia's faith, if not her heart."

Dawn was smiling, a soft misty smile. "And didn't he capture your imagination, Gale?"

"I've met men like that before," I said shortly.

"Gale, you've fallen for him," she said in a gently irritating singsong.

"Nothing of the sort. I've only known him twenty-four hours, and then met him on the scene of a crime, where his presence—mind you—has not been satisfactorily explained."

"You don't really believe he kidnaped Bette, do you?"

177

I tried to push my emotions out of it, answer honestly. "I don't know. Whoever executed this plan was either so ingenious or so naïve that his cleverness—or simpleness—has gathered up the trail behind him. Someone met Bette as she got off the school bus, put her in a car, and drove away. That's all. No one noticed the car or took the number, so there must have been nothing unusual-looking about the car, neither too old nor too elegant."

"But where did they take her? Where?"

"If I can find Cora Mears, I may know the answer." I crossed the room to where my camel's-hair coat was lying on the divan. The all-weather coat I'd worn the night before and in which I'd thrust the gory scarf was now in the cleaners. I lifted the big coat, found a handkerchief, and thought of something else—the fact that I never carry a purse and Dawn carried such a big one.

"Do you have a permit for a gun?" I asked Dawn as I came back to my place near the window.

"No." She was lighting a cigarette and didn't look up. "I don't, but Geoff gave me a revolver, told me to get a permit for it. I meant to, but so much has happened. You know, it's very lonely here along the river. That little park across the way is deserted at night and I walk my dog down there. One night I was followed."

"What did he look like—the person who followed you?"

"It was a girl. It was the last night Geoff was in town, the day before I got the letter from Eddie. Geoff and I had been out to dinner. When we came back, Geoff had some phone calls to make and as Leila, my maid, was off, I took the dog out. I walked across the street in that little park by the river. It was a cold, still night. There was no one else about. Then I noticed the girl. I thought at first she was waiting for someone, then I realized she was watching me."

"It's no fun to be shadowed by an amateur," I said, remembering Bart Crane's footsteps that night on Third Avenue.

Dawn frowned. "I'm not sure she was following me, exactly. You see, I didn't pay any attention to her at first, so I don't know if she was waiting in front of the apartment or came along after I was on the street. But there have been so many holdups over here. I thought she might have been a lookout."

"Sort of a finger girl," I said. "A spotter for the mob. They do have them."

"Whatever she was, she frightened me. I ran dragging Simba on his leash. He's a poor coward of a pup and would probably have been too scared to bark. I fell in on Geoff practically in hysterics. He went down right away but said there was no one in sight." She sighed. "He gave me the gun then, told me to get the permit, but next day I got the letter from Eddie, and you know how things have been since."

I knew. I picked up my fresh drink, walked to the window, looked down on the river. A tug scooted by. Over in Long Island City, factory windows glowed red with reflected sunset, red as blood. The day was nearly done; so was the case. All my brief high hopes were sunk. Every lead ended in a blind alley.

So I knew Cora was a blonde. So what good did it do me? It proved nothing beyond the fact that she might have been there. It still might have been Sylvia . . . or

179

Dawn. She had a slick explanation for the gun, but no evidence of the truth.

Somewhere a telephone rang and the maid appeared, said it was for me. By way of contrast, Patsy's shrill voice greeted me.

"Oh, Gale, that Lieutenant Deery was in the office, and is he mad!"

"Where are you now?"

"Home. I was just leaving the office when he walked in and said he wanted to see you—right off. I didn't take any chances, even calling from a phone booth. But don't you go to your apartment, if you don't want to see him. I'm sure he's parked right outside."

"Thanks a lot, Patsy. I'll stay clear until I'm ready to see him."

Then in a hoarse whisper she said, "Is Miss Ferris there? I bet her place is beautiful."

I put my hand over the mouthpiece. "It's Patsy, your number-one fan."

Dawn said, "Bring her up to tea sometime. I really mean it."

"I'll hold you to that," I said, and repeated the invitation to Patsy. There was a deep silence, a deep sigh, and the click of a telephone. Patsy had evidently collapsed in a trance. But remembering Tess Miley, I was thankful for Patsy. At least she had no ambition to be a kept woman.

There was no larceny in Patsy's soul, nor could I believe there was much of it in Dawn's. It was the stupid greedy people like Cora and Tess who wanted everything for nothing and drove little men to desperate deeds. And perhaps Sylvia—that would be grand larceny

180

—handsome Sylvia who couldn't have married middle-aged, eccentric Theodore Alexander for any reason but money . . . or pity. And Sylvia wouldn't pity easily.

In a dark mood, I drifted back to the window. This hour the night before I'd been looking out over the rooftops from Bart's studio. If only I could stop thinking about him! If I could only stop thinking! I turned abruptly, surprised Dawn in staring at me.

"You don't want to give in, do you?" she said.

I shook my head. "But I haven't a chance of a break now. And yet I feel so sure that the answer is close—like a word on the tip of your tongue. Dad used to say there weren't any perfect crimes, only imperfect policemen. I guess I'm just a careless cop."

Dawn switched on the lights, bringing out new and lovely tints in the big room. Then she rang for the maid, gave her some instructions. I stood by the little bar, nibbling on peanuts, while my thoughts kept spinning in a dark whirlpool.

"I still think the answer is in the Alexander home," I said, half to myself. "It must be. The police and the FBI have checked everyone there, each person's history and contacts. Those boys are thorough, and yet Eddie knew the murderer, so did Wurber, and their only other contact in life was when your child was placed for adoption. Wurber knew Sylvia, but he didn't really know Cora."

Dawn was prowling the room, stopped before me with a question. "Do you think that Sylvia would have planned this to get the estate—particularly if Bette is—isn't really her child?"

"I doubt it. But it might have been planned one way

and worked out another. There has to be a man in this somewhere, and it may be Cora's rich man with the car. Noah Taylor, Sylvia's father, kept insisting it was someone in that house, and I think he was right. Half right, anyway." Hugging my elbows, I was pacing the floor when Leila wheeled in a tea cart trailing a fragrance of warm food.

Dawn laughed as I turned around quickly. "You probably haven't eaten all day," she said, "and for that matter, neither have I. Leila has turned us out one of her heavenly omelets and hot muffins. You can't think on an empty stomach."

"Thanks for the reason," I said, "and I really am hungry."

Swiftly Leila set a small table for us, lit the candles, brought the coffee. Dawn was very pleased. "Isn't that nice? I know you'll feel better." Then she had another idea. She put a stack of records in the radio-phonograph. "Now you won't even have to talk."

It really did help—the luxuriously restful room, the good food, the lovely music. After a delicious dessert, a second cup of coffee, and a cigarette, I was decidedly improved, and Dawn was purring.

"I'm so glad you liked it," she said. "You did me a favor. You know after all the years I've lived alone I still hate to eat by myself. I swear that's how I've kept my weight down. When Geoff and I are married I'll put on tons."

"A lot of women feel that way. I've never minded it particularly, but it is nicer to have someone share with you."

What was it Hank Deery had said about cooking

breakfast for a good man? He wouldn't be so amiable when he finally caught up with me. Dawn was still talking about the problems of the woman alone.

"That was one reason I was glad that you called me this afternoon. I never expected you would, after what I did, but I wanted desperately to know what was going on. And then," more lightly, "I wanted a drink and I can't drink alone. Always makes me feel guilty. Probably just shows my age, but how girls can go in bars by themselves . . ."

"They do it. Mike Nash, the barman over at Dario's, hates to have lone girls hang around the bar, but what can you do? Monday night, when Bart and I were in there, I noticed a girl . . . a girl . . ." I kept repeating slowly, like a stuck record, then I was on my feet.

"Dawn, that girl who followed you over at the park! What did she look like?"

"I don't really know," she said slowly. "She had on a hood or a wool wimple, you know—that covers the head —and a dark coat. It was a very cold night. I think her hair was blonde. She was tall and young."

"Was she good-looking? Was she unusual?"

Dawn shook her head helplessly. "I don't know. I can't remember. She walked . . . Oh, yes, her walk was rather unusual."

Dawn sprang up, her head high, her shoulders set, as if she were getting in the mood for a role. She hesitated thoughtfully, then got my camel's-hair coat, put it on, belting it tight. She crossed the room with a square-shouldered sort of lurch, a tense sexy kind of swing, and her lovely face took on an expression to match it—a boldly sullen look.

With a shout, I hugged her to me. "That, my pet, gets all the Oscars for the season. Oh, Dawn, Dawn—it's perfect now!"

"Whatever do you mean?"

"The woman who waited for you in the park, the girl in the red raincoat at Dario's, who practically spit in my face, the blonde who went to see Eddie—they're all the one person—and her name is Cora!"

18. AT almost seven-thirty I walked into Dario's. I looked around the place quickly, saw no one either familiar or suspicious. It was a good time. The before-dinner drinkers were gone, the after-dinner drinkers hadn't started. The few who remained were either in a hurry or too far gone to be observant.

I slid on a stool at the end of the bar, nodded to Mike, who was mixing double Martinis for a pair of far-gone ones. He got to me as quickly as he could.

"That was a fine-looking man you were with the other night, Gale," he said approvingly, and then, "What'll you have?"

"An apricot brandy will do." I only wanted an excuse to talk to him. When he returned with the liqueur I said, "So you liked him?"

"Indeed I did. He has a look of class to him. Was it only business?"

"Strictly, Mike," I said, too sharply, "I want to ask you something about that evening. While Mr. Crane and I were here, a girl in a red raincoat came in—a tall blonde girl with square shoulders."

Two new customers occupied Mike's attention momentarily while I played with my drink. Two others wanted repeats. My finger tips ached with tension. Any second Deery or one of his men might walk in—men I'd known all my life and with whom I'd have to go quietly, if unwillingly. Mike finally drifted back, casual and good-humored.

"About that girl, Gale, she wasn't with you?"

"No, Mike. She came in alone and sat at a table near us in the back. She left when we did and she said something to me there in the entry. It was raining. Remember?"

Mike leaned his big paw, clutching a towel, on the edge of the bar and scowled. "A big girl—would you mean with a big mouth?"

⋅"Definitely with a big mouth," I said, then to make it easier for Mike, "a broad mouth, amber eyes—cat color—and golden hair, a good figure. I think," I added, "her name is Cora."

Instantly Mike beamed. Why do they call them the women that men forget? They never forget them—they may not marry them, but they don't forget them.

"Oh, why didn't you say Cora? I remember her."

"A neighborhood character?"

"Oh, no. She hasn't been around long—maybe since Christmas, I can't be sure. And no regular, really. I haven't seen hide or hair of her since Monday night."

My palms were sweaty. "Mike, did she ever come in here with a little guy, much older but kind of cute?"

Mike served two double Martinis, a beer, and a straight rye while he was thinking back and I was dying by inches. He looked absolutely woebegone when he returned to me. "I'm that sorry, Gale, but never do I remember when she wasn't in here alone. It's something's worried me—a beautiful girl like that and always alone!"

"Where does she live, Mike?"

His rather handsome Irish face was blank. "Indeed, I don't know. For all I ever ask, nobody who comes in here has a place to sleep."

"Mike, look—I've got to find this girl."

It was almost eight. The double Martinis were in again, also two Old-Fashioneds—favorite cocktail of assignations—and three beers. The beer trade was definitely arriving. Mike came back with a worried look.

"Gale, you know if I could help you . . . In fact, I'm very flattered that you come to me . . . I only said to Libby this morning, any time I could help Gale . . ."

"Mike, you could help me now, if you'll just remember."

"I don't know! Cora comes in, she drinks her drinks, she goes out. And me, now," he added with sudden virtue, "I'm not like some bartenders in this town. I don't make dates for my customers."

"I don't want a date with her!"

One of the beers wanted a refill. Another customer arrived. The bar stool seemed sprouting pins and needles. Suddenly Mike rushed back to me, a fresh-drawn beer in his hand that was definitely not mine.

"I just remembered something. I sent her over to Hiller's liquor store across the street."

"So?"

"They deliver! Maybe Hiller got her address."

I was on my feet, forgetting the untouched drink, the unpaid bill.

"Tell him I sent you," Mike called after me.

I lit across the street toward a small brightly lighted store, with a small brightly polished little man in attendance. He greeted me as though he expected a two-case sale.

"Mr. Hiller? Mike sent me—Mike Nash at Dario's."

"He did? What can I do for you?"

"A favor, right now," I said, and his nice smile didn't dim, which to my mind is top salesmanship. I told him briefly about Cora. He looked faintly unhappy.

"We can't give out customers' names and addresses."

"I know her name. It's Cora Mears, or Cora Wells. She used to live in Pottstown, Pennsylvania, and here in New York she was over on West Seventieth Street for several months. But I lost track of her and it's very important . . ."

Mr. Hiller was smiling again. "Well, you really do know her, don't you? But you can see our position . . ."

"Indeed I can," I agreed heartily, "and only that you're a friend of Mike's, I wouldn't ask."

"And he did send her to me," Hiller admitted. "A very nice customer, I must say, but rules . . ."

A patrol car stopped outside. I turned my back to the door, concentrated on Mr. Hiller while chills crawled up my spine. The door opened and the cold air had a personal meaning. Then a hoarse voice said, "Joe been around tonight?"

I trembled with relief as Mr. Hiller shook his head, dismissed the inquirer, continued to smile regretfully at me. I turned on all the winning appeal I could find.

"I do admire a man who runs his business on such high principles. If I were a customer of yours—as I

188

well might be any time now—I wouldn't want you giving out my name."

"You never know why people want such information," he said chattily. "Now the Fletchers—from whom Mrs. Wells sublets—they're very different. People are always stopping in, asking about him. They're in California now. He's a writer—Fletcher, I mean."

"Donald Fletcher, the mystery writer?"

"Yes, indeed. Do you know them?"

"Of course, I have autographed copies of his books. I should write and thank him for that last one. I must look up his address."

Mr. Hiller, impressed with his own cleverness, was twinkling at me. "It's either Five-ten or Five-sixteen," he said gaily. "I'm not sure of the number, but I do remember the name of the apartment. I've lived around here all my life. It's the old Gordian Arms."

"Thank you so . . ." I began, when my mind was caught in one flash of memory. There was Sister Anastasia at St. Clare's, teaching ancient history. There was Bart Crane sitting comfortably in a big chair, nursing a drink and discussing the peculiarities of old Mrs. Alexander, who named her real-estate purchases in honor of the life and times of Alexander the Great. And didn't Alexander cut the Gordian knot?

"You said Gordian Arms?" I repeated.

"That's right, near Second Avenue, next to the Olympia. They used to have the names spelled out in leaded lights over the door—very swank at one time."

"It must have been beautiful, Mr. Hiller, and how about sending me some liquor?" In sheer gratitude, I ordered a case of assorted stuff to be delivered next day, then headed for Lexington Avenue on the double. From the first phone booth I called the Alexander house in Huntington.

The voice that answered sounded like my old flat-footed friend Wilson. I asked for Mr. Taylor. After a moment's delay, his unmistakable snarl responded. He recognized my voice, too.

"Well, hello, now. How did you make out? Been thinking about you."

"I did all right. Anybody home?"

"Nobody but Wilson and me. Sylvia ain't come back yet, and neither did Baxter. He phoned this afternoon, seemed more worried about Sylvia than Bette. Nothin' for me to do but chew m'nails down to the nubs. Did you find out anything?"

"I found out a lot, Mr. Taylor, thanks to you, and now I want something more. I need some information about the Alexander property."

"Property? Crisawmity, they own half o' New York. I don't know much about it."

"Ever hear of any apartment houses named the Gordian Arms and the Olympia?"

"Sure, sure. That's theirs. The old lady named 'em out of history or something. Ain't had a vacancy in one of 'em since thirty-nine."

"Know anybody named Fletcher?"

A moment's hesitation. "Can't say I do. If I met 'em the name don't stay with me. But don't go foolin' around with no strangers. I tell you this is an inside job. Nobody listens to me. . . ."

"I do, Mr. Taylor, and I'll be seeing you soon—with Bette, I hope."

190

I walked out of the store and east toward the river. That wasn't a casual comment to Noah Taylor. That was a vow.

I walked fast down the dark block. I was excited because I was sure—dead sure—that this was the end of the trail. Gordian—that was what Eddie was saying on the telephone and Bart mistook for guardian. Gordian was the word Wurber was trying to write. The apartment belonged to the Alexander estate, so they—someone in the family—could arrange a sublet during the housing shortage. And the woman behind it all was Cora Mears.

All that seemed clear—but with whom was Cora working on this thing? Everything pointed to Sylvia. Perhaps she had palmed Bette off on Theodore Alexander as his own child, and now that he was dead, she was using the child as a tool to get more money. The estate would certainly put up the cash for the ransom, and she may have figured a way to grab it for herself. If that were the case, Bart Crane was her accomplice.

My dark train of thought was interrupted by the sight of the name "Gordian Arms" on the fan glass of an old apartment building. It had been, as Mr. Hiller said, swank; but the big lobby had been stripped of the rugs, lamps, and lounges that undoubtedly once adorned it. Reduced now to its essential marble and tile, it looked like a station rest room without an attendant.

The large board in the entrance with its call buttons and speaking tube had no doubt supplanted the original switchboard and telephone operator, just as the self-service elevator had further helped to reduce the house staff. Knowing how these places are run, I assumed

191

they had only a superintendent and a porter, neither in sight at that hour of the evening.

I studied the names of the tenants on the board. Fletcher was listed as 5C. In the lobby I spotted the C line of apartments, in the northeast corner of the building. I took the elevator to the top floor, walked the remaining flight to the roof.

Rooftops are very important to Manhattan apartment dwellers. Here tenants—depending on the economic scale of the house—hang their wash, do their home dry cleaning, take their sun baths, and sometimes do their courting. Anyone who has ever lived in one of these buildings knows the way to the roof unerringly. In the chill spring evenings the roof had not come into its own as a community center. Except for some baby wash, flapping in the wind, there was no sign of life as I stepped out into the night.

The sky was faintly overcast but at this height the glow from the great vivid pulsating city below created sufficient light for me to find my way around the vents, chimneys, and unexplained hazards as I made my way to the northeast corner of the roof. A break in the parapet marked the entrance to the fire escape. My hands in my gloves were cold as I gripped the iron handrail and began the descent.

It was a good firm fire escape as such things go, but still it vibrated with my every step on the open metal treads. Looking down I could see there was no light in the sixth-floor window leading to the fire escape, but one could never tell what moment someone would walk in that room, and spot me in that light coat, a large bright target in the night.

The steps, I discovered, came down on an angle with the upper pane of the window so that the shade cut the view of the fire escape. However, I had to pass that breadth of window facing the landing in order to reach the next flight. From the brightly lighted windows of neighboring apartments I could have seen the silhouette of any person watching me. But those in darkened apartments had me at an advantage. With each step, I was sure a thousand eyes must be on me, though one treacherous pair would have been enough.

I crouched down, slid cautiously past that sixth-floor window. Once on the other side, I peered over the sill. From a light in the hall beyond, I could see the outline of a bed, the glow of a mirror, in what apparently was a small rear bedroom. I continued my cautious progress down to the fifth floor. There was no sign of light there, either.

After a full minute of waiting, while I steadied myself, I edged up to the window. The room was totally dark. I saw only a hazy reflection of myself in the pane. The window was closed. I took a quick look with the flash where the sashes joined. The catch was not set. I used a coin for leverage, got the window up, slid my hand, palm out, into the room, and set off a clatter that almost toppled me backward on the fire escape. I had struck dark Venetian blinds drawn down to the sill. I stood flat against the wall, waited. There was no sound from the room.

My experiences at house breaking the night before were still too fresh in my mind to give me much zest for daring. The memory of Dawn's frantic warnings and pleadings when I left on this mission didn't help either. But I couldn't risk being too late this time. Kidnaping carried the death penalty. I couldn't forget that it would be simpler to dispose of a dead child than to conceal a live one. Ruthless people were playing a desperate game, and if they became panicked . . .

The continued silence in the room reassured me. I sat on the sill, swung my legs up, braced myself as I leaned under the Venetian blind, found the pull cord. Careful as I was, the slats rattled like dry palm fronds in the wind as the blind rolled up. Still holding the cord, I dropped my feet to the floor.

Reflection from the street highlighted the room. The decor helped. It had a modern treatment, dark walls and white woodwork, so that I could spot the door, which was closed, and the other window, also closed with blind drawn. Then I was aware of the stale smell of the room, an overpowering combination of soiled clothes, food, and perfume. Quickly I tied up the blind, left the window open for ventilation and escape, then turned my small flash over the room.

As in the apartment upstairs, this was a bedroom, furnished in modern style, with Swedish maple, circular unframed mirrors, dark carpets. Judging from the furnishings, the place was much better kept when the Fletchers were in residence than by their tenants. In the brief arc of light I got an impression of terrific disarray, cups and glasses on the dresser, soiled clothes on the floor, the bed unmade. Suddenly I caught an image in my mind, like a still from a motion picture. That bed . . .

I turned the light again, and followed it with infinite caution. The bed was tumbled, the sheets soiled, no case on the pillow, but there across the quilt was an arm . . . a slim, white arm, a long-fingered hand, grubby, with dirt under the nails.

My stomach knotted with tension as somehow I made my feet move forward, inching across the carpet. I reached out a shaking hand and touched the other one. It was cold. I pulled back the quilt and the arm fell aside, a head came into view, a head with tangled chestnut hair, and a small face, unbelievably pale, a face with winged eyebrows and an uptilted nose. My heart seemed to stop altogether.

There in the bed was a little girl, and her name was Bette Alexander.

19.

I KNEW a flash of prayerful exaltation as I bent over the child, but I had little time for emotional didoes. Things had to be done and quickly. I went to the door, listened. There was no sound. I didn't know the plan of the apartment. It might be the railroad type, with the living room almost half a block away, or again all the rooms might open on a small inner hall, which would increase the possibility of any sound being heard. I had only one aim—to get Bette out of there.

Quickly I pulled the covers off the girl. She was long, lean, and limp. She wore only an old rayon slip several sizes too large for her, which kept sliding off when I tried to sit her up. After two tries I gave up, began chaffing her thin wrists and chill feet, even slapped her lightly. She only rolled her head away, mumbled faintly. In the general mess on the bureau I found a cup of cold tea. At least it was wet. I soaked a handkerchief in it, wiped her face. She obviously hadn't had a bath since her abduction—the previous week—so that the tea ablutions only made her more pale.

The room was chill and fresh now with the window wide open, but I was sweating. I had to get Bette out of there, but she was much too big for me to carry. I had to start her going under her own steam. Once I had her out of this apartment, even to sit on the fire escape, I'd raise the neighborhood, and Deery could have his case.

I leaned close to her, whispering, softly, insistently. "Bette, wake up, hon. Bette, come now. Bette . . . Bette . . ." She stirred, collapsed. I went through the same routine, wondering if I could take a desperate chance of leaving her and running for help. But they could do away with her, swear she was never there. Obviously she'd been kept under heavy sedatives for a week, and no other tenant in the house knew of her presence.

"Bette, Bette," I kept on earnestly, while my thoughts ran in wild circles. If I took something for identification, closed the window and the blind . . . "Bette . . . Bette . . ."

Her eyelids flickered. I leaned closer to her. Groggily she looked up at me, moistened her cracked lips with her tongue. "Cora . . ." she murmured faintly. I was thankful she was too weak to make a racket.

"No, this isn't Cora. I'm a friend, Bette, a friend of your mother's, of Gramp's, of Bart . . ."

"Gramp . . . Bart . . ." Her whimper, like that of a small sick child, tore at my heart.

"You must get up, Bette. I'm going to take you away from here . . . take you home."

She retreated, her thin body digging into the mattress. "No . . . no."

"Please trust me. I've come to help you."

"No," she murmured stubbornly, even as her lids sagged again.

I was mentally wringing my hands. I took her thin

shoulders, shook her. She tried to push me away but had no strength. I got my arm in back of her, forced her to sit up, then had to grab her before she toppled forward. With my free hand, I snatched up the cup of cold tea. If I could get her to swallow! I held the cup to her mouth but she set her lips tight, turned her head. She made a real effort at that.

"No, no!" she muttered through clenched teeth. I put the cup aside. Perhaps she was right. They may have been giving her sleeping medicine in liquids. The poor child was certainly doped to the ears.

I went on with my strange battle there in the half-light, coaxing, pushing, pulling, pleading. Finally I got her feet over the side of the low bed. The moment I let go of her she fell back, but I found sox in the clothes on the floor, put them on. I rummaged around for a sweater, found a pajama top.

Once more I sat her up, made loops in the straps of the slip to hold it on, then worked her limp arms into the pajama sleeves. Her eyes were staying open a little better now, and she drank in the cool night air thirstily. All the time I kept up my whispered encouragement.

"In a few minutes now, you'll be all right. I'll take you to Mother and Gramp."

"Gramp," she echoed foggily, as if reaching for something lost in memory.

My hopes crept up. She was coming around slowly, but she was coming. I got her to her feet. Her legs promptly folded and I had to start all over again. With whispered cheers I steered her to the window. If I could only get her out on that fire escape landing and shut the window behind me, I was going to let out a yell that would blast the neighborhood.

It couldn't have been five feet from the bed to the window, but it seemed like the last long mile. When she did get a bit of strength, she used it to resist me, pulling back like a mule, her eyes open now, but not focusing very well. My hand had touched the window sill when the door banged open, light filled the room, and striding toward me was—Cora.

"What the hell goes on here?" she demanded.

Bette promptly collapsed on the floor. I made a dash for the fire escape, a shriek coming up from the base of my diaphragm, but Cora's big hand clapped over my mouth and she whirled me around. Taller than I and powerful as a blacksmith, she sent me spinning across the room like a top. Quickly she slammed the window, dropped the Venetian blind, accompanying herself with a stream of polished profanity.

Braced against the wall, I drew my gun. "Suppose you show me to the telephone, Cora," I said. "You're all through."

"That's what you think, you dirty snoop. I told you to stay out of this."

"And your advice tipped your hand, and led me right to you—and Bette. Now we want out—quick. Come around here, your hands locked over your head, and show me the telephone."

I wasn't fooling at all. I always thought I couldn't use a gun if it came to a showdown, but I could have done it this time. Cora moved across the room with that walk Dawn had mimicked so perfectly, knees slightly bent, hips swaying. Her wide mouth quivered with fury, her cat's eyes darting and suspicious.

"Into the hall," I said, motioning with the gun.

I moved away from the wall then, turning slightly in line with the door. As I did, the corner of my eye caught a flash of motion. It was a finger reaching for the wall switch, just inside the door. Two things went through my mind, fast as tick and tock—the person that should be, the person it could be—Bart Crane. But even as I thought it, I fired.

There was an oath, darkness, and a clout in the side of the head that lit the room for me personally. The gun was knocked from my hand. I ducked as another blow whistled past me, slipped, sat on the floor hard. The light went on again. Cora, leaning against the cluttered bureau, had the gun, a smirk of satisfaction on her face. The man was standing in the doorway. Slowly I made myself turn and look up at him. It was—as I so desperately hoped—Montgomery Baxter.

"Funny how we keep running into each other today," I said, getting slowly to my feet. "I suppose you don't want *the family* to know about this either."

Baxter's eyes blazed, the unctuous voice was choked with fury. "The family—that cursed family! All my life I've bowed to them, done their dirty work, been their errand boy. I couldn't get away with anything . . . not even any little thing. But now I've done it. I got back. I got mine."

"I think you've yet to get it," I said, moving backward toward the bed. Bette, over by the window, was struggling to her knees, looking at us in bewilderment.

Baxter leaned against the door. "You don't really think they're going to stop me, do you?"

"I'm sure of it," I answered, lying like a lady, while my spirits rose unaccountably. I glanced at Cora. "So this is the rich man who's going to keep you?"

"We're going to get married," she said.

"A legal life on illegal gains. Besides, he does have a wife and two daughters in Brooklyn, a very nice wife, too."

"I know all about that," she snapped. Baxter said nothing.

"You certainly pick the crumbs," I went on. "Eddie Wells, then this."

"Eddie Wells was nothing to me."

"Merely your common-law husband for six months." I glanced at Baxter. He looked confidently contemptuous. Apparently he knew all the bad news about her and didn't care. I couldn't get them fighting with each other, as I had hoped. I sat on the side of the bed and looked up at him.

"So it was you who killed Eddie and Wurber, you who knew that Bette was not Sylvia Alexander's child."

At that moment, Bette had reached the bed from the opposite side, dropped across it, and clutched my hand. Cora snapped: "Leave her alone."

Baxter waved Cora to silence. "It doesn't matter, sweet. They're not going anywhere. I got the money from Crane—fifty thousand dollars."

"So you did get it," I said, my hand tightening over Bette's cold fingers, my heart mounting steadily, in a sweet rhythmic tattoo. It wasn't Bart . . . it wasn't

Bart. . . . I even managed a smile. "Darn clever, aren't you?"

Baxter was bragging now. "Of course I'm clever. The Alexander family depended on me for years for everything. When Sylvia Alexander found she couldn't have a child and her marriage was about to blow up, it was I who arranged the deal with Wurber. Without my help, she couldn't have put it over on Theodore Alexander. They were already separated, but when she told him she was going to have a baby, everything was made up—and stayed that way."

"That ought to have paid you well over the years."

"They never appreciated Buzzy," Cora said.

Baxter nodded. "Cora's right. Sylvia promised if I'd swing the baby deal, she'd open the house in Huntington again, see that I had a job for life." He made a derisive sound. "Sentence for life!"

"So it curdled," I said, looking at him but rubbing Bette's thin hands, trying to keep her awake, though I didn't let myself think for what reason. Baxter was too busy pouring out his accumulated grievances to notice us.

"Yes, it curdled. Sylvia treated me like an office boy. When Theodore died and I asked for a decent settlement, she said she didn't have anything. When I threatened to tell the trustees that she bought this baby, Sylvia said go ahead. She'd tell them that Theodore knew it wasn't his child—and it would be her word against mine."

"So you cooked up the bright idea of snatching the child and getting the ransom?"

"I had a perfect setup," he said defensively. "And then Eddie Wells came back. He was the only one who

202

knew that this child was not Sylvia's—he and Wurber. He had simply followed Wurber's nurse from the hospital with the baby. Eddie came back . . .'' Baxter glanced at Cora but went on talking, "and he wanted money. He went to Wurber, and the doctor sent him to me. As long as Eddie knew, I thought he was perfect.''

"Perfect, hell!'' Cora snapped. "Eddie was a weak-minded fool. We'd have been in the clear if he'd gone through with it.''

Suddenly Bette said: "Eddie! I like Eddie. Where is he?''

"She knew him?'' I asked.

Cora nodded with impatient contempt. "Buzzy had her meet Eddie several times, when he brought her in town to that artist. The idea was that she'd get to know him and go with him when the time came.'' She laughed. "The idea was good, but Eddie, the silly fool, fell in love with the kid and backed out on the deal.''

Poor Eddie; the one courageous act of his life had ended it. But Cora had no pity, only swaggered a little as she continued: "I didn't let Buzzy down. I drove the car and picked her up myself. She knew me, too, and I told her I was taking her to Crane.''

"But before that, you'd transferred from Eddie to—Buzzy?'' I grinned ruefully as I used the name.

"There was no comparison,'' Cora said stiffly, and Baxter actually beamed.

Looking at this precise, fussy man, I tried to picture him in the role of archcriminal and failed. Right then he was gazing fatuously at Cora. For men she must have had the face that launched a thousand ships, but to my disenchanted eyes she was just a greedy tart. Then

203

I remembered Edna Baxter, so neat, so prim, so cool, and the grim, morguelike reception room of the Alexander house, and had a swift flash of understanding for this man who had found all the wealth and all the woman he ever wanted.

"So Eddie threatened to stop the whole thing," I said slowly, "even tried to give it away after the kidnaping. You found out he telephoned Crane and you shot him—and then I walked in."

Baxter's moment of happy glory vanished. With a change of expression so startling that it practically constituted another face, he swung from Cora to me. "You . . ." He had a word for me. "You upset everything. There never would have been any connection between Eddie Wells and the Alexander case if it hadn't been for you. Sylvia would never have dragged Wurber into it again. I had everything fixed."

Baxter laughed unpleasantly. "I even got another letter through and arranged the pay-off. I warned her that no one in the house was to know. Sylvia took the directions so seriously, she didn't even tell me. She gave the money to Crane that very morning you came. That was the beginning of the end. You'd contacted Bette's mother and I didn't know who she was. Wurber didn't know either."

"I told Buzzy," Cora tossed in flippantly. "Eddie was always bragging about his beautiful wife. I went over to get a look at her. A pale blonde. But I didn't even know she was Bette's mother until after the snatch. I thought maybe Eddie had a lot of wives. But I helped, didn't I, Buzzy?"

"You helped before, you're going to help now." He

moved into the room. His revolver had a silencer on it. The *Kaffeeklatsch* was over. There was an icy spot in the pit of my stomach. Every minute counted, every minute that we were still breathing, still holding out, but Baxter was done with stalling, impatient now.

"You always made things hard, Miss Gallagher," he said, moving toward me. "Bette's been too groggy to be aware of anything up to now, but you had to change that. Now she knows too much—and so do you."

Bette, her fingers digging into my arms, began to cry. "Be still, Bette," I heard myself saying.

"She will—right away," Baxter replied.

His arm shot forward and so did mine, throwing Bette back on the bed. She let out one long terrified shriek. I lunged headforemost, caught Baxter in the belly. He staggered against Cora but didn't drop his gun. I threw a chair between us. Bette had rolled off on the floor, and was pounding and screaming with rising energy. Cora snatched a pillow and leaped for the child. I was aware of the sudden, awful silence as Baxter came toward me, as I crouched behind the chair.

"Close range is safest," he said.

The shot shook the room. Automatically I huddled flat against the floor. As the reverberations died away, I realized I wasn't hit. A bit stunned, though, I reared up slowly on my knees. Baxter was swaying, clutching his arm, slowly crumpling, like a second figure in a ballet, descending as I rose. Then I turned my head slowly, blinked as Hank Deery walked in the door, followed by two very capable-looking gents, one of whom grabbed Cora.

Hank crossed the room quickly, lifted Bette. Her

skinny body in the weirdly assorted clothes sprawled in his arms. He laid her on the bed, felt her pulse, seemed satisfied.

As I got unsteadily to my feet, Hank shoved his hat back on his head, looked me over coolly, and said, "Where you been all day? I've been looking the whole town over for you."

At my exasperated gasp, his grin softened into a gentle smile. "Your old man would have got a bang out of this."

20.

I WAS late going to the office next morning. I took time out to read the papers, answer a few dozen telephone calls, send my beat-up clothes to the dry cleaners, and get my beat-up spirits in working order.

It had been a victory—a big triumph; and yet I couldn't throw off a heavy feeling of defeat. I even coddled myself and took a cab downtown. For a routine trip to the office such luxury gives me a guilty conscience. But after a fee of two thousand bucks for four days' work, I really could afford a cab, and, as with many New Yorkers, it's my pet extravagance.

I also wore my tan gabardine suit—a slick tailored job of which I was very proud and fond—and the beaver jacket. There undoubtedly would be photographers, and this outfit always helped my morale. Why my morale should need help at this point, I didn't know. I should have been on top of the world. Everything had worked out so beautifully.

Flashes from the previous evening still whirled in the background of my mind like a montage. There was, of course, that first bow from Deery, which for me was the Congressional Medal, the Croix de Guerre, and the Apostolic Blessing all rolled in one. That bouquet also took a bit of the curse off his explanation of how he trailed me, right straight from Mike Nash at Dario's, to Hiller, to the apartment. It also helped my pride that he got started on that trail with a direct tip from Dawn, who had phoned him after I left. Altogether it evened things up. No detective is the one-man marvel he likes to think he is.

Besides, there had been such a rumpus in the apartment that the tenants both above and below the Fletcher domicile had called the cops. I had beaten the police on the punch to Cora, and even I hadn't been a minute too soon. Baxter had planned to give Bette an overdose of sedative and leave her in the apartment for the Fletchers to find on their return from California in April. By that time, he and Cora expected to be comfortably settled in South America, beyond the reach—they hoped—of American justice.

There was also that unforgettable scene of joy and tears that Dawn and Sylvia staged—a pair of old scene-stagers from 'way back. Best of all, to me, was the sight of Noah Taylor striding into the suite at the Waldorf that Sylvia had managed to corral for all this, and Bette flying into his arms. It made you wonder how much blood relations really do count.

What I didn't see but couldn't forget was the way Edna Baxter must have received the news of her husband's crimes. There was a string of them against him— murder, kidnaping, adultery, and a little plain chiseling under the name of Brock. Edna Baxter would be older this morning—a great deal older—with her neat little world in pieces.

Perhaps it was the thought of her that made me sit like a limp rag doll as the cab rolled downtown. Or it could be reaction, I told myself. It had happened before in lesser degrees, but then they were lesser cases. You get keyed up, lose all perspective, all sense of time and values. It was the kind of thing men must experience in war, a kind of ecstasy in danger shared. Persons you've known only a few hours become important out of all relation to time and experience. It's hard to let go.

At the office, I managed to perk up and make an entrance that would have done no discredit to Dawn Ferris. As I suspected, two photographers and a reporter were waiting for me. When I finally got inside, Patsy rushed to greet me, her eyes shining, her lipstick on crooked.

"Oh, Gale, you were so wonderful! And a man named Marty White called and says he has forty dollars for you because Cute Copper came in in the sixth. And Gale," she lowered her voice and took on the drooling look, "he's here."

"Who? Marty White?"

"No! I know I shouldn't have let him in your office, but he was so sweet to me. Such a gentleman! I could tell right off he wasn't a reporter."

"That would fix you with the press," I said, scooping up my mail and heading quickly for my office to see what Patsy had let me in for now. I stopped abruptly on the threshold. There, seated at my desk, calmly regarding the traffic on Fifth Avenue, was Bart Crane.

As I recovered my plunging poise, he turned on his most ingratiating grin and came toward me, hand outstretched. "I just wanted to be the thousandth to congratulate you," he said, his handclasp warm and steadying.

"You're very kind. Everyone's been very kind," I murmured, as I slipped off my jacket, tossed the mail on the desk, glad for any action to cover my mounting nervousness. He walked around the office, pretending not to notice.

"I stopped in to see Bette this morning," he said.

"How is she?"

"Coming along fine. She wanted two breakfasts. I suppose with two mothers, she'll want everything in doubles."

"What are they going to do about that two-mother situation?"

"Sylvia and Dawn saw eye to eye on that right away. Bette will stay in the one home she's always known, but Dawn will be welcome at any time. Incidentally, the Alexander estate is planning to reward you rather handsomely."

"I've been rewarded. Dawn Ferris paid me well and Hank Deery topped it." I glanced at Bart, hesitated because I always find such things hard to say, but he looked so expectant I had to finish. "Hank said my father would be proud. That meant a lot."

"I'm sure it did," he said gently. "I'm sorry I wasn't in at the finish, but I was at the district attorney's office."

"On the ransom?" I asked, as I dropped into my chair, faced him across the desk as I had faced Dawn only five days earlier.

"Partly." He locked his long fingers, regarded me mockingly. "It seems that all branches of law enforcement look askance at a painter—house painters excluded."

"I was not suspicious of you because you were an artist," I insisted.

"It was sufficient cause for the police. I don't know if I made it clear to you, but they questioned me very relentlessly during the first forty-eight hours of Bette's disappearance. They seemed to think my profession placed me just one step above vagrancy, and the ransom furnished sufficient motive. I'm sure only my Navy record saved me from immediate arrest on suspicion. So it was not only my fondness for the child but a bit of personal pride that made me work with them so closely."

"Work with the police? I thought you were working with Sylvia."

"I was working with Sylvia, but she didn't know I kept the police informed of what we were doing."

"Then you did tell them about finding Eddie's body and my being there?"

"I had to report the finding of the body and I didn't know what you were doing there. If your story was straight, you needed to be warned to stay out for your own protection. If you were lying to me—as I suspected —a little investigation was in order."

"But what were you doing outside of Wurber's house that night?"

Bart shook his head. "That was really a bad time. As you know, when Eddie came east, looking for big easy money with which to hold Cora, he went to Wurber, who, in turn, sent him to Baxter. When Eddie found out what Baxter was planning, he reported back to the doctor. Wurber really wanted nothing to do with it."

"He certainly didn't," I agreed, "but as long as Wurber knew, that cut him in, according to Baxter."

"And Baxter was going to be sure he was in. That gentleman wanted plenty of company in case of a hanging. When the first attempt at collecting ransom failed, Baxter came up with a second scheme."

"He didn't give up easily," I said, reaching for a cigarette.

"It was the old lion-by-the-tail situation," Bart said, leaning forward to light my cigarette. "He couldn't let go. He had Bette on his hands. As he planned it first, it was going to be a quick job. He would get the money and skip. Life had lost its flavor. He wanted a lot of money—and freedom. By the old system of two sets of invoices—one for himself, and one for the estate—he'd been getting a little extra money for some time, but he wanted a lot."

Bart lighted his own cigarette. "Then he saw Cora and he wanted her, too. Even with Eddie out of the picture, Baxter figured they could still get away. But Eddie wouldn't stay out—so he died. At that point Baxter still planned to return the child if he got the money."

"And he did get it," I said.

"That was where he rung Wurber in. I was to leave the money, stuffed in a pair of work shoes, with the counterman in a lunchroom on Broadway. A fellow named Bill would call for them. Then I was to meet Wurber, who would take me to Bette. I was to wait opposite his house for Wurber to come out. I left the money at the lunchroom, took up my post across the street, and you know the rest."

"You must have been surprised to see me go in," I said, able to smile about it by then.

"Surprised is a definite understatement. The kidnaper himself might have been in there at that moment. We know now that Baxter had been there half an hour earlier, found Wurber so jittery that he endangered the whole plan, so Baxter killed him."

"If I'd been a little earlier . . ." I shivered.

"Yet you walked in so confidently, I thought you were there by appointment."

"Perhaps I'm in the wrong business. I should be working with Dawn."

"It's an idea," he said, crushing out his cigarette on the big metal ash try. I followed the motion of his hand. My eyes suddenly widened. He, too, followed my glance, raised his arm, and inspected a reddish thread of stain on the rim of his dark blue coat sleeve.

"That mark," I said. "I noticed one exactly like it on the sleeve of your gray coat in Dario's."

His eyes twinkled. "Sorry to disappoint you, but it's paint. All my sleeves are marked that way. I go back to put a touch on a picture, something else is not quite dry . . ." Laughing, he rose, and right then I thought of something else.

"Those conferences with Baxter at the Phrygian Club before the kidnaping. How do you explain those?"

"There were no conferences with Baxter. He wanted a place to pick up messages after office hours, so I gave him a guest card to the Phrygian. He was already known there because Alexander had belonged to it. Theodore Alexander, Senior, and my grandfather, Lucius Bartley, founded the thing, sort of an expensive poet's corner at the time.

"The original Phrygians lent some left-wing aid to a Greek campaign, and the whole Alexander clan was touched on this subject of the revival of Greek culture. Baxter was using the club as an excuse to his wife while he visited Cora."

Bart reached for his hat—that awful battered number. "It's a beautiful day, Gale," he said. "Must you work?"

I rose, too. Suddenly I felt very gay and lighthearted. "I should—but there are still a lot of things I'd like to ask you."

The desk was between us but something in his gaze made him seem very close to me as he said softly, "There are a lot of things I want to tell you."